THOUGHT CATALOG BOOKS

Andrew

Andrew

M.J. ORZ

Thought Catalog Books

Brooklyn, NY

THOUGHT CATALOG BOOKS

Copyright © 2016 by M.J. Orz

All rights reserved. Published by Thought Catalog Books, a division of The Thought & Expression Co., Williamsburg, Brooklyn. Founded in 2010, Thought Catalog is a website and imprint dedicated to your ideas and stories. We publish fiction and non-fiction from emerging and established writers across all genres. For general information and submissions: manuscripts@thoughtcatalog.com.

First edition, 2016

ISBN : 978-1945796081

10 9 8 7 6 5 4 3 2 1

Cover design by © KJ Parish

To my wife, Megan, as always.

The devil on your shoulder has a name...

Contents

Acknowledgements

To Richard Orzechowski, Jason Carter, Brian Snyder, Brady Janorske, Andrew Padgett, Bryan Ziolkowski. You guys keep filling my head with horrifying ideas. Don't stop.

1

Magazines

I had a hard time falling back to sleep after the first time my sister tried to smother me. I remember it as thinking that maybe she was just playing a game or something, but once I realized that I wasn't going to be able to get any more air into my lungs, the game was over and this was an attempt at murder. She pushed her pillow so hard against my face that it made my cheekbones swell for the week after the attack. My eyes were black from her elbows shoving the pillow down onto my face while she pinned down my arms with her legs, all of her weight sitting on my pinched throat. I remember my chest feeling like it was burning and blood rushing to my face before passing out. Thank God my sister is too damn dumb to know the difference between passed out and dead.

I told my parents every time it happened, which is something like four, maybe five times now. Every time I did they gave me a puzzled look and told me I must be dreaming. When I saw my sister at the breakfast table, she pretended as if nothing happened and, even though my neck, cheeks, and eyes were swollen, it seemed that everyone in my household believed that it was nothing more than a dream. My sister would never do such a thing. I must've fallen out of my bed–which I admit had happened in the past, but never to the extremes of my injuries and not since I was maybe six or seven years old. I woke up when I fell. I know what it is like to fall. This was not a fall. This was my sister, eleven years old, two years younger than me, trying to snuff out the light from eyes. I simply refused to give up the ghost.

It was just before my fourteenth birthday that I ran away. It was frightening at first, but after a week or so, I grew used to it. I tried my best to stay outside of town–any town–and would walk for miles every day, much of it along railroad tracks and through wooded pathways until I ended up someone else. Eventually every location I ended up started to be new to me and unfamiliar. After about three weeks of being on the run, I began to understand that my family was not going to look for me. I pieced everything together in my head and realized that my parents knew what my sister was doing. They had to. They were just letting nature take its course, as terrible as that sounds.

I say this now with such ease because the world is much more clear to me. I say this now because I have learned. The games my parents would play that involved me staying in the locked cupboard weren't games at all. I wasn't amazing at hide and seek. No, I was kept out of the public eye. I wasn't allowed out or to make any noise when family came over. In fact, I recall not being able to ever meet my family when they came over; grandparents, uncles, aunts, and the like. I never got any Christmas gifts from them or from my parents or from anyone, honestly. I was allowed to exist. This would explain why my father would call my mother a whore and refer to me as 'her kid.' To that respect, I guess it is a stretch to call my father 'my father' then, isn't it? We can refer to him as Jacob from here. Jacob and my mother did not provide for me like they did my sister and did not give me the same privilege in any manner–my sister's attempt to kill me were only the final straw in decision to leave. And they didn't want to find me, so now, finally, I could start over and become my own man.

Though my past was a bit more traumatizing, and I may have had more struggles spending my adolescent years out on the streets and in the woods, making tents from stolen blankets from Wal-Mart and eating what was thrown out in the dumpster of the shopping centers. The best time to start looking, by the way, is around nine in the evening. Many of the shops close at ten and start taking out the trash at nine. If they see you, sometimes they will bring you out food or, at least, give you the leftovers before it makes its way into the dumpster. I was still pretty typical in my following of pop culture. I would steal one of those celebrity magazines and look at pictures of all the actors and actresses on the covers and I would read all about how awesome their lives were. If I could be anything, especially when I was that age, only sixteen years old or so, I would've been one of those movie stars in the magazines. I could wear the tuxedos to all of the big events and drink expensive alcohol and pretend to give a shit about the environment, just like they do. I could've done whatever I wanted because I would have had all the dough and the guy with the dough calls the shots. Even just to get my face on the cover of one of those magazines would set off my career and I would be the head guy in charge of everything. That's just how the world works, whether you like it or not. It's not until you're on the cover of some magazine that people start paying attention to what you have to say.

So I was traveling east, I believe, somewhere around the

Appalachian Mountains, when things started going badly. I ended up walking through the city limits and hopped into the back of this eighteen wheeler that rattled down the highway and stunk to high heavens. When the truck stopped, I hid behind one of the boxes, but it wasn't long before the driver of the truck found me. Before I knew it, I was in handcuffs and being brought to the police station in a city called Hagerstown. It didn't take long for them to find out who I was, where I came from and, being that I was only sixteen, start making arrangements for me to get back to my parents. I refused to go, but they informed me that they were on their way and that they would be able to pick me up in the morning, being as how they were only a state away. They put me in my cell and told me to get some sleep and just like the nights where my sister tried to put me out of my misery, I had a hard time keeping my eyes shut. For the first time in two years, I couldn't fall asleep.

In the morning my attention was quickly fixed on the noises I could hear down the hall. I placed my head close to the bars to hear Jacob's voice hollering about where his kid was and wanting to know what he had done wrong to end up 'getting thrown in the slammer.' The door to the hallway opened and in walked Jacob and my mother, both of their eyes set with fury. The officer released me to them and we all sat in the car silently for about forty-five minutes before Jacob decided to speak up.

"What the hell did you think you were going to do?" he asked me, never separating his teeth. "Where the hell did you think you were going to go?"

"I was gone for years and the two of you never even bothered to find me. I've been all over the place. And I don't need to answer any more of your questions."

"You'll do as I say, boy. I'm not going to play these stupid games with you. Your mother and I have been having enough stress at the house without you being there and we certainly won't put up with your lip, do I make myself clear?"

"Good to know my sister's okay," I said, sarcastically. "Glad to see you still haven't given up on her yet."

"She's a good kid, Samuel," Jacob said to me, not taking his eyes off the road. "You wouldn't know anything about that, so drop it."

"She was a bitch," I replied, sharply. "Just like the both of you."

The car pulled over to the side of the road and came to a stop. Without a word, I saw Jacob turn around and, with one long swing, bring down a black club of some type across the top of my head. I was out before the pain had time to set in.

———————

I woke up to what sounded like sirens going off inside of my skull. I could hear it all resonating, bouncing around my brain, making the process of waking up almost unbearable. I grabbed my temples and rolled over onto my knees, pressing my forehead against the cold, wet soil. Lifting my head, I took a look around to see a blur of brown and green. My vision was slowly coming back and, even though it hurt like hell, I stood to my feet, only to slide back down onto my bottom. I placed my hands over my bent knees and waited for the world to come into focus.

Trees. Lots and lots of trees. And dirt. That's all I could see. There was a downed log over in the distance, but beyond that, everything seemed pretty uniform. Just leaves and bark for as far as I could see. I ran my hand over the top of my skull to see what the damage was. A huge knot sat right on the top of my head, making me feel as though I probably looked like one of the cone-headed alien folk from the movies. It hurt to touch, but when I pulled my hand in front of my face, there was no blood, which I was very thankful for. The blow was hard enough to knock me out, but not enough to split me open. I sighed a belated breath of relief and chuckled for a second. That bastard Jacob must've thought I'd be dead by now. Jokes on him. Asshole. I'm not dead yet.

Once my vision cleared and the headache began to go from a sharp edge of pain to a dull roar, I stood and decided it was time to begin searching. For what, I don't know, but I needed to find something–anything–that could help me get back to civilization. I figured I couldn't be too far from a road or a path that Jacob could've driven on. He was a strong guy, but not really strong enough to drag my limp body for more than half a mile, I would assume. But then, I don't want to underestimate him and his determination. I know if I was hiding a presumably dead body, I could probably get it out into the woods quite a distance. Regardless, I needed to get back to something that would guide me home. Wherever home is going to be from here on out.

I carefully place each step in front of me, making sure not to stumble, holding on to the trees that I passed as I made my way over to a fallen log. If anything, it would be nice to be able to sit on something besides the dirt to think about my next move. I reached the wooden corpse only to realize that much of it had began to rot, I pushed my hand down onto a spot that looked soft only to be proven right as my palm cracked the bark and landed inside the log. Even at two or two and a half feet in diameter, this thing was surprisingly soft. I walked along beside the log until I found a section of it, down by the base towards the roots that were mangling themselves into the air, which was tough enough for me to sit. Though it was not initially comfortable, I was able to wiggle around enough on the tree to find just the right nook to make this wood somewhat worth my walk over. I put my weight on my hands, leaning back a bit and let out another deep sigh.

"You seem tired," a voice said from below the log, causing me to jump to my feet.

"Who the hell said that?" I hollered, throwing up my fists, causing myself to topple a bit before catching my balance. "I swear I'll fuck you up! Where are you?"

"Calm down, please," the small, humble voice said. It was only then that I realized the voice couldn't belong to anyone older than a child. It was too meek, too tiny for anyone who was actually grown. I put my fists at my side and called out to it.

"Are you okay, kid? Where are you? Are you hurt?" I said.

"I'm not hurt," it replied. "I'm just lost. And scared. Are you hurt?"

I laughed at this, stepping closer towards the noise, which seemed to almost come from the log itself.

"Actually, I am, just a bit though. I'll be all right. What are you doing out here? Do you happen to know how to get back home?"

"This is my home," the young boy said. "Right here."

"How can this be home? There's no house, little guy. Are you playing a game?"

"No," it said back. "Would you like to play one?"

"Do you know where I can find a road or a house or maybe even a phone?"

"Who would you call, Samuel?" the boy asked.

I stopped and took a step back, my fist clutching once again at my side, growing ready to fight.

"What did you say?" I asked.

"I asked who you would call?"

"You know my name. How?"

"Because the man who left you out here was screaming it while he dragged you out here. He said you were a bad boy and some type of stupid little fuck. He also said that he would see you in hell."

To hear this small of a voice use such harsh words made my stomach hurt. I don't know quite why I was sensitive to hearing something like this–these words were not new to me by any stretch of the means–but to hear them come out of a child left a bad taste in my mouth, which combined with the rather eerie thought that this child had watched Jacob pull me out here and leave me to die.

"How long have I been laying there? When did that man leave? Which way did he go?" I asked the boy, who still hadn't revealed himself.

"He left a long time ago. He was really mad and pretty scary. Not too scary, though, because I don't scare very easily. You were laying there for a really long time though. And he went that way." A small pale hand came over the log and pointed in a direction opposite of which I had started walking. The tiny white hand shook slightly and didn't remain pointing for long before retracting back behind the log. "Are you going to leave?" it asked me.

I crossed over towards the log, making sure that my footsteps didn't make too loud of a noise, even though this kid was completely aware of my presence. It gave me the feeling like when I was very young and would chase squirrels in the backyard. I would tip-toe towards them, silently, and even though I never caught them, I truly believed that if I was quiet enough, I could be successful.

"Do you want me to stay?" I questioned in response. "Would you want to come with me?"

"I can't," it said back. "I can't leave."

"What do you mean?" I replied. "You can come with me. At least until I get back to a town or a road. Why don't you come along?"

"I said I can't."

"Well why not?"

There was a pause that gave the air a cold, looming sense. I felt like the breath that wanted to make its way into my lungs was hanging in front of my face instead of pushing itself down my throat.

"I'll show you if you come here," the boy said, softly.

I kept my cautious stance as I crept towards the tree. Inch by inch, through the thick, thick silence I moved closer and closer until I was standing with my knees pushed against the bark. The boy said nothing as I leaned over, peering beyond the horizon of the log. What I saw shocked me to the core. The boy, lying on his side, was not only pale, matching the complexion of the hand he had offered up just minutes prior, but seemed sickly and diseased. You could see his bones through his joints and it seemed as though he had been there for weeks. His clothing was tattered and torn, barely hanging from his emaciated body. On his ankle was clasped a shackle, almost like what you would see in the old movies. It was about two inches thick, rusted, and covered by the raw, rubbed, and chaffed skin above this boys foot. It was obvious that he has pulled against the chain and had failed at freeing himself many times. The chain ran from the shackle up to the tree and seemed to be rooted into the tree itself. The boy looked at me, fear and concern pouring from the brightest blue eyes I had ever seen.

I immediately jumped the log and grabbed the chain to help the child, but it wouldn't budge. My head was throbbing as I yanked on the chain, pushing my foot against the log and trying to force the wood to crack.

"It's not going to work," the boy said. "I've tried that. It has to be my foot."

"What?" I asked him frantically, still pulling the chain. "Who did this? What is going on? How long have you been here?"

"It has to be my foot. The chain won't break. I promise."

"I'll go get help! Which way was it to the road?"

"The road is miles long and I don't have that kind of time."

He said all of these things with such calm and such patience, like he had accepted death already and was willing to go into the light. It was almost like he just wanted to go. Like it wasn't a big deal.

"What do you mean it has to be the foot? Like, you have to slide it through the loop?" I asked.

"You have to take off my foot. Or break it. I can't do it. I'm not strong enough and I'm scared. Break it and slide it through."

"I can't do that! No! Hold on! I'll get you loose!"

"Break it," he said back, still collected and calm. "Just one quick snap."

Tears ran down my face as I pulled the chain with every ounce of strength I had, giving forth no results. I pulled until my shoulders hurt and my knees cramped over.

"Please, God, no." I said to the child, who still stared at me with the oceans behind his eyes. "Please, no."

"You have to break it. Please. Do it."

"I can't!"

"Please."

The boy shut his large blue eyes and put his face to the earth, his hand dropped to his side as consciousness slipped away from him. I had very little time to help this child if I wanted him to make it. I don't know what caused me to be so compelled to make sure he was ok, but I felt the need to get him out of there–to get him to safety. I counted to three in my head and with a trembling hand I grabbed his foot and pushed the toes down to where they would straighten out with the leg itself. There was a quick pause as the tendons tightened, but I kept pushing until a final, loud snap was heard. The boy stayed asleep as I slipped his mangled foot through the shackle, before stepping aside to vomit in the leaves beside us both.

When I came up for air, I was horrified to see the boy, standing above me, his ankle no longer broken, his clothes no longer tattered, his size back to what could be expected of a child his age, and a smile creeping across his face.

"You did it," he said to me as I quickly scooted away from him. "Congratulations. I'm very proud of you. You did well."

"What the fuck is this?" I shouted, shaking furiously. "Is this some type of trick? It can't be. I swear I just broke your...I know I just broke your ankle. I heard it. I felt it."

"I know you did! And I am glad you were able to muster up such courage. What a brave young man you are. You've done so well. I think you're going to be great."

"Stay away from me! Go away, you...you demon!" I kept sliding myself away, but every time I would pull my body across the mud, this boy-devil-thing with the blue eyes would follow me, at my pace. He towered over me until I finally hit my back on a stump amongst the leaves. I covered my face and waited for pain. But none came. I let my hands go to rest after a moment to realize that the boy was sitting in front of me, crossed-legged and smiling, but not the sinister smile he had from before; a kind, sweet smile. He smiled like he actually cared about me and wanted me to be happy, even in my terror.

"What do you want from me?" I asked.

"I want you to be the star you always wanted to be," he said.

"What?"

"I know what it is like to lose a dream," he told me. "I know how hard it is to do those things you want in life and how unobtainable the stars can really be when your feet are planted here on Earth."

"Are you going to hurt me?" I asked him.

"No." The boy chuckled briefly. "Quite the opposite. I'm going to help you, Samuel. I'm going to help you get your face on the magazines, just like you always wanted. Isn't that what you always wanted?"

I looked to the ground, wondering how much of this situation was real and how much of it must have been caused by the crack to the head I had taken from Jacob's club back in the car. This had to be some kind of messed up, deceiving brain trick or dream or something, I thought. It couldn't be real. The boy sat there, waiting for me to answer, grinning.

"How are you going to help me?" I said to him, more curious about playing along with the story now than figuring out what in the world was going on; what was real and what wasn't.

"I'm going to make sure that you get on the magazine covers you always wanted to be on. I'm going to help you become the celebrity you always idolized. I owe you that much, wouldn't you think?"

"Why do you owe me?"

"You saved me," he answered. "I would've died if not for you. I would never have gotten free if you didn't come along and help me. I owe you this. I owe you your dream. So I am going to help make you famous." His head tilted over towards his shoulder and, again, he chuckled. "What do you think?"

"What do I have to do?" I asked him. "How do you plan to…"

"Just trust me," he said, cutting me off. "And do exactly what I tell you."

I listened to the boy. I heard every word he said and I can remember agreeing with all of it. He told me all about how it wasn't my fault that I wasn't amounting to anything–no, he reminded me that I was doomed from the beginning. My family was awful. My upbringing was terrible. And this boy, Andrew, I remember him saying his name was, made sure that I knew that it wasn't my fault. None of it. And that the only way for me to get the notoriety that I wanted to was to first get rid of that family that held me back for all these years.

He was right.

I got the notoriety after I burned down my childhood house. I got the fame and my face on the cover of the magazines, just like I always wanted after I took that club to Jacob's head just before lighting the match. I locked all the doors and barred them with furniture. My name will always be remembered, just like Andrew told me it would. And tomorrow, I get to be the biggest star of them all. They all get to watch me sit in that chair, looking at them all through the glass. They get to watch the poison take to my veins. They get to see my final bow before I am immortalized as a legend. The nation will be watching.

And I owe it all to Andrew.

2

Let's Play Truths

I hated everything about this place before I even got here. There was nothing in this world worse than having to pick up and leave everything behind, which is exactly what happened to me when I was about twelve years old. I had a small group of friends back in Baltimore and the idea of having to move on to middle school without them was killing me. I wasn't the same kid without my friends. I wasn't going to have anyone to relate to–to share things with. I certainly wasn't going to be happy anymore. I could feel my social world, even though I was far too young to really understand it, slipping away from me as my parents drove along the narrow road that split the cornfields of eastern Maryland. Everything from here on out was going to be terrible.

My mother believed that it was best that we wait until summer to move, seeing as how it would give me a good transition into a new home. I was wrapping up my elementary school days and they probably believed that it would be a lesser agony if I started in a new school when I would have been doing so anyways, just in the suburbs of Baltimore as opposed to the middle of nowhere that was Redvale. They had my best interest in mind and now, as I am older, I can see that, but it was unclear to me as a child that that was their intention. I thought they were pure, unadulterated evil.

"Don't worry, dear," my mother would constantly tell me. "It'll all be fine. Just give it a chance." I would shake my head at this and never actually give her any response. It would not be fine. It couldn't be.

I went to school on the first day with my same blue JanSport backpack that I had used the previous year in elementary school. It wasn't as fun or exciting as the other kids in my old school who had various cartoon characters and superheroes on their bags, but I love this backpack. It was a bit too big for me, but I could carry everything in it and, to be blunt, it was mine. I didn't have many things that were "mine."

My mom and I didn't move to the eastern shore on a whim. There was work out here and the housing was relatively cheap if you were in the right town, away from the boating and marinas and the ocean. If you found yourself smack dab in the middle of the DelMarVa Peninsula, just like Redvale, then you could find yourself a place for just the right price. And my mom did just that when things started going south at her job. Work wasn't easy for her to find anyway in the state, but this was a small sacrifice for the amount she would get in return. To them, it was more than worth it. However, even with this in mind, and even though she made things work, we were not a family of money. We didn't have many "things" as a family, and I had next to nothing that was "mine." But that backpack was "mine."

I enter my first classroom of middle school, nervous as can be, double checking the homeroom sheet they had given each student just a few days earlier in the mail. The room number was B403 and I must have looked at the tiny plaque on the wall a thousand times to be absolutely sure this was the right place. It was. B403. The teacher, Miss Smith, stood smiling behind her desk, politely ushering students into the room. She appeared to be friendly enough, but there was certainly something fake behind her smile. I believed, and still do now, that every teacher is a nice teacher on the first day. That is how they reel you in. The board behind her read "Take a seat!" which gave us the obligation to find the desk with our name tag on it, that I assumed we were supposed to put around our necks with the yarn that came attached to it. I put my backpack on my chair and placed the name tag with "Matt S." around over my head. Moving my backpack to the floor, I took a seat and waited for the rest of the class to file in.

A slew of kids rushed through the door in small groups, separated by gender and obvious athleticism. I was anxious to see who would be seated in the grouping of desks I belonged to and hoped that they were kids I could get along with. As I waited, watching the door, I heard a scraping sound from the side of my desk and a blur crossed my vision.

"My backpack!" I cried. I watched my bag slide across the floor, hooked onto the ankle one of the larger boys. Without a word, the boy stopped, looked down to see what was slowing his pace, and kicked feverishly to release himself from the grips of my pack, breaking the shoulder strap in the process. "Hey!" I shouted. "That's my backpack! Stop!"

The boy grinned and I could feel his laughter before it left his mouth. My gut turned to stone as my eyes peered around the room for the teacher to see if she was there to save me, but she must have stepped out into the hallway to corral the other children in. This husky boy was now laughing at me as he kicked my backpack across the room, right up to my feet.

"Watch where you put your crap, new kid!" he said to me as other children began to laugh along. I watched him put his name tag around his neck. "Ben." His name was Ben. I had been in this school for only about fifteen minutes, and already Ben was going to make sure that my life for the next three years would be miserable. Miss Smith reentered the room, hushing the crowd of sixth graders, and began introductions. I felt like I was holding back tears for the entire forty-five minutes until the bell rang.

I started down the hallway, my now-busted backpack slung over only one shoulder, looking at my itinerary to see where my next class was going to be. I had only taken a few steps before I felt a strong tug from behind yank my whole body from the pack. I almost fell over completely but was able to release the strap from my shoulder before I lost my balance.

"Just trying to even those straps out for you, dweeb!" said the voice behind me that I knew was going to be all too familiar before my career at this school was over. I turn to find Ben standing over me. His fat gut stuck out from his slightly small shirt and I could feel his warm breath, stinking around me as he held my backpack over his head. "Let's see what little-twerp has in his bag!" With this he began to empty the contents of my backpack all over the floor of the hallway as I scrambled to save my books and folders from flying too far away, as if it would save me from even further embarrassment. The others around us in the hallway snickered as they walked by, one even kicking a book of mine. Whether it was on purpose or an accident, I couldn't tell, but my guess was that it was intentional. I was able to collect my materials just as Ben dropped the sack in front of me, still on all fours, just about to come up from my crawl.

"Come on!" I cried out, making the other kid's snicker go to a full on laugh. I went to stand but was quickly pushed back onto the tile by Ben. "Let me up, Ben!" I said, trying to get up as he held his hand on my shoulder, his enormous weight keeping me grounded. With a jerk, he released me and I flung my body up and down the hallway without turning around. I could hear them all making fun of me as I left. I felt their fingers pointing at me. They may as well have been firing rounds into my back. Luckily, I did not have Ben in any more classes. I ate lunch alone. I stayed away from people the best I could. I hated my new school. I hated this stupid town and everyone in it.

When I got home, my mother was in the kitchen, getting started on dinner, pulling the chicken out of the fridge to thaw. She saw my face and could only assume the worst. She offered the obligatory, "How was your day, dear?" I did not give any reply. I simply went to my room and took my books out, placing them all on my bed, seeing as how the rest of my furniture hadn't yet been assembled. I went back downstairs to my mother and asked if I could go for a walk. She looked worried at such a request, but I think out of sheer sympathy she allowed me to leave, reminding me to be home by six for supper. I nodded and headed out the screen door, jumping off the rickety porch without touching a single step.

I didn't know where I was heading. I didn't know the area at all. I had a few hours before I had to be home, so I figured that, if worst comes to worst, I could always just turn around and retrace my steps if I felt as though I was getting lost. I wandered out beyond my neighborhood and past one of the giant corn fields that were scattered all over this town until I came to a gravel road that lead into a thicket of woods. The dirt of the road had been driven on, but I could tell not by anything recently. The trees around the road seemed to form a tunnel that curved off into the green and brown depths. It was quiet along this path and, even at only ten years, I enjoyed the solitary sense of peace that came along with this little patch of land.

I wasn't sure if this place belonged to anyone–if it was on someone's property–or if it was just a forgotten road that led to, apparently, nowhere, but I continued until I could hear the trickling of water. I followed the sound until, just through the clearing of trees, I could see a wooden structure connecting two ends of a ravine. It seemed to be some sort of bridge, but unlike anything I had seen before. This structure had a roof over top of it that left an enclosed tunnel through which the wind howled. Just big enough for a small car to fit through, but not structurally sound enough to hold that much weight from what I could tell. I couldn't imagine anything continuing down this road with this thing standing in its way. I thought this was the end of the journey and, as I looked up to find the sun, I believed that it should be the end of mine, as well. I turned, slouched, and kicked dirt with each step until I heard the voice of what seemed to be another child.

"Why are you so sad, friend?"

I spun around quickly to see where the voice had come from but found nothing around the covered bridge or inside the tree line. I wanted to run, but I was enveloped in anxiety and fear which held me in place.

"It's all right," the voice continued. "You don't have to be afraid of me. I'm not afraid of you."

"Where are you?" I shouted. "Show yourself! Right now!" I twisted my head around frantically, trying to see if anyone was going to appear, but nothing came from the woods.

"Come here," said the voice, now sounding desperate and lonely. "I'm not going to hurt you. I just want a friend, that's all."

"I'm not going anywhere! Where are you? I'm going to call my big brother down here and he's going to kick your ass if you don't come out from your hiding spot. I'm serious!" I hoped this kid didn't call my bluff. I definitely didn't have a big brother and, even if I did, I doubt he would come down and kick some random kid's ass for me. I stared hard towards the bridge, looking for any type of movement when finally I was able to see a small patch of brown rise up from the ravine under the bridge. I noticed the brown was this boy's hair, obviously cut by an amateur, maybe his mom, which was shortly followed by bright blue eyes that stuck out like turquoise from the earthy ground he rose from. He stopped just as his nose came over the dusty horizon of the ravine.

"No need for that," the boy said.

"I swear, I'll go get him if you don't come out from behind there. I'm not playing with you. He's big and…"

"I meant no need for the lying," the child replied. "You don't have a brother. You don't need to threaten me. I just want to be your friend. Don't you want a friend?"

"I'm not lying!" I called back, trying to sound scary as opposed to expressing the embarrassment that ran through me.

"No. You are. It's okay. Please stop. Come here."

"You don't know me!"

I took a step back and just as my foot touched the ground behind me, the kid spoke, still softly.

"You're going to want to stop walking."

I took another step backwards, not breaking eye contact.

"Stop walking."

Another step.

"STOP WALKING!"

The rise in the boys voice caused me to shake as I stood, now obeying his word.

"Turn around and look down," the boy told me, his face still half covered. "Turn around and look."

Reluctantly, I followed his command and jumped backwards towards the covered bridge My chin hit my chest and I saw what was just a foot or so behind me. There, loosely coiled, was a brown viper, its head raised from its body, waiting for me to take another step towards it. The diamond patterns on its back warned me of its poison–something I learned from my parents in a book they had shared with me about animals growing up.

"How did you know that was there?" I hollered, trying to keep my vision between the boy and the snake as balanced as possible. Two seconds on one. Two seconds on the other. Neither one moving. Both equally as horrifying to me in this moment.

"I saw it," giggled the child. "Just like you did…eventually. Come here. It is safe here. I just want someone to play with. My name is Andrew. How old are you?"

I watched the viper slither off into the woods, now making

it safe to keep my focus completely on Andrew. I turned completely on my heel, as fast as I could, to see that he has yet to move from the first spot he had appeared in. I was standing closer to the ravine now so I could see a bit more of his face. He looked just like a normal boy. As I approached him, I realized that he was not only obviously younger than me, but significantly smaller, both in height and weight. If anything I could see about this kid, or rather know about him without even having a conversation with him, it was that he very well might have been the only kid in this town who needed a friend more than I did. I could tell this just from his size alone.

"I'm twelve," I told him. "I'll be thirteen soon. My name is Matt. Why are you sitting in the ditch?"

"It's quiet down here," he replied. "Would you like to join me?"

I stood overtop of him now, looking below covered bridge. I could see that the boy was standing on a few rocks that had been stacked along the wall of the declining earth. He must have placed them there so he could see over the edge. The ground in the ravine was dry and covered with leaves from the early autumn chill, even though it was still September. Putting my chin up as not to show fear, I sat down and slid on my bottom into the crumbled orange and red below. I stood and looked to the boy who was standing with his hands behind his back. A beaten-up pair of dark overalls shrouded his small form. He had on a white T-shirt under them, and I could guess that this boy did not come from a household of money. He looked me up and down and I returned the favor. After the inspection I walked over and sat down next to his pile of rocks.

"Why don't you have anyone else out here with you? This seems like an awful far place for someone like you to come out to alone."

"I could say the same for you," he retorted, his gaze now fixated on his feet in front of him as he sat down beside me. "Where are all of your friends?"

"I don't really have any," I told him. "I just moved here not too long ago. My family is still getting used to things. I'm sure I'll have plenty of friends, though, once I get to know people more. I just started the sixth grade, so I have three years at this school to get to know people."

"You're lying again," he told me. "I asked you to please stop lying to me."

"I'm not lying!" I said, beginning to grow frustrated.

"You are," said the boy, now tapping his toes together in his dirty canvas shoes, his heel dug into the dirt. "You don't think you're going to make any friends and it scares you a whole lot. I know the feeling. It's okay. I don't have any friends either. I think that's why we found each other."

"Shut up!" I yelled to the boy. "You shut the hell up! You don't know me at all and I'm leaving. I don't want to be your friend!"

"I would be the only one you have."

"I told you to shut up!"

The child looked up at me and, for the first time since our confrontation, I noticed the scar that ran across his right cheek. I couldn't tell from looking at it what had happened to him, but whatever it was, it definitely looked painful. The scar was around two and a half inches long, running vertically down his cheek, almost touching the corner of his mouth.

I wanted so badly to ask what had happened to him, but wasn't about to start another casual conversation with this kid. Instead, I stomped my feet up the side of the ravine and trudged my way back up to the dirt road that led me to the bridge in the first place.

"I'm going home," I yelled down to the boy without turning around to see if he was looking back at me. He didn't reply. I walked through the woods, back out to the main road, and eventually back home, now shaken and quite angry. My mother asked what was wrong, but I didn't bother telling her what had just happened.

———————

The boy from the bridge haunted my waking and sleeping. I thought about him every few minutes and wondered if he was still at the ravine. I knew this was a stupid thought and knew that, at some point, he had to have gone home, but I think I wanted to believe that he was some sort of troll, living eternally under that bridge, coaxing children in, possibly to eat them or something stupid like that. I thought about him when I was in school and even asked some of the kids if they had ever seen him around before, drawing nothing but laughs from my fellow classmates. A boy in overalls who sits inside a ditch is not exactly something people really were familiar with and certainly was not something that they wanted to chat with me about. I chalked the lack of responses up to the idea that maybe this child was homeschooled and not registered in the normal middle school, which would make it even more believable that he didn't have any friends.

As this fact loomed over my head, I began to feel sympathy for him. I thought about how hard it was for me to make friends and he didn't even have the same opportunity that I had if he had to be schooled at home. If he had any brothers or sisters at home, they obviously didn't like playing with him or he wouldn't have been sitting in the ditch all by himself. The more I thought about it, the more I wanted to go back to the bridge to see if maybe he would be there again; to see if maybe I could give him another chance. Maybe we could even be friends. I knew I could use one.

I decided that day that I would go back out to the ravine and search for the kid, even if just for a few moments to see if he was still sitting on his pile of rocks. If not, I could always say that I tried and I think I could live with that. I would have tried. The best thing I could do. I didn't even make it out the front door of the building when I heard the crashing of a trash can behind me. I look down the hallway to see if there was a teacher around to save me, knowing very well what was going to be coming my way in just a moment. No one. Not an adult in site. I gulp and move my head over my shoulder, praying silently to myself that it wasn't what I thought it was coming up behind me.

"'Sup, asshole!" Ben cackled, stomping his gorilla like feet in my direction. "Where you going? Back to Mommy?"

"Ben, not now," I said. "I really have to get going." I tried walking away, but he caught me by the shoulder before I was able to get out of his reach. Without thinking, I smacked his arm off of me and, almost as if by instinct, shoved him as hard as I could in the chest, knocking him down the ground. I look around once more. Nobody saw it–teacher or student. Then I realized that no one was there to save me. Again, teacher or student. Ben stood angrily, his nostrils flaring, his fists clenched tight. Without doing the cautious search around the hallway like I did, he reared back his hand and with one swing clobbered me in the face, knocking me out for a second or two.

When I came to I could already feel my eye swelling shut. He had hit his target dead on. Ben stood over me, a smile on his face.

"Don't ever think to try that shit again. Understand me, dweeb? Next time, I won't be so gentle."

Ben spit on me as he walked off laughing. I stood up, brushed myself off, and took a minute in the boy's room to cry in privacy.

———————

When I finally made it to the dirt road, my eye was completely blackened out. There wasn't any blood, so I was grateful that it didn't make a mess of my clothes–I feel like that would've only upset my mother even more and I knew she was going to go on a tirade when she saw my face. It was strange only being able to see out of one eye. I felt off balance and like the world had shifted just a bit. I worried that it was going to still be around for school pictures, which were only a month away. I knew that if I had this giant welt in the photograph, my mother would be enraged. I would have to listen to her tell me how I should've been more responsible and how I should've been around a teacher if I was worried about being bullied at school. It was embarrassing to think that she would probably be up at the school tomorrow to speak with my teachers anyway, but for now, I wanted to put all of that aside and focus on the task at hand.

I found myself in front of the bridge again, looking down under the wooden pylons, trying to find the small boy.

"Andrew!" I shouted. "Andrew! Are you here?"

"Yes." I heard from behind me, making me jump. "Welcome back, Matt."

"I thought about what you said to me. I felt bad and stuff, you know, and…"

"I know. Come on."

Andrew slid down the hill and found his place on his normal stack of rocks. He looked up at me, then down to the ground beside him, as to gesture me to sit. I slid down with him and got myself comfortable.

"Your eye looks like it hurts." Andrew said to me, looking down to his shoes, just as before. "You should have gone home first, you know."

"How do you know I didn't?" I replied, smugly. "Maybe I did."

"And you brought your backpack and didn't bring ice or anything for your swelling. I don't think so. You came straight from school. I can tell."

"How old are you, Andrew? You're too young to be thinking…"

"I'm older than I look." Andrew said, cutting me off. "I'm sorry you were hit. I've been hit before. It's not fun. It looks like it'll heal up in a few weeks."

28

"Is that how you got that…well…your…"

Andrew nodded.

"Something like that," he told me. "So are we going to be friends now?"

"I suppose. Is there anything you like to do?"

There are lots of things that I like to do. Would you like play a game?"

"What kind of game?" I asked.

"We can play Truths." he suggested, proudly, finally looking up at me with his shining blue eyes. "Do you like Truths?"

"I don't think I've ever played before. What is it?" I asked.

"It is essentially like Truth or Dare, except it eliminates the dare portion. I think it will be a good way for us to learn a bit more about each other. What do you think?"

I didn't quite know how I felt about this boy and his game, but I figured that, at this point, I had nothing left to hide, so what harm would it do to, essentially, have a conversation with the kid?

"Fine. We can play Truths. You first."

"Okay." Andrew said. "Who was the kid that did that to your face?"

I paused, now looking to my shoes, much like Andrew had before.

"His name is Ben and he's an asshole. He's just some big dumb bully at school."

"You don't like him, I take it?" Andrew asked.

"That's two questions. Is that how the game is played?" I responded sharply.

"No. Good catch. I'm sorry. Your turn. Ask me a question."

"Where do you live?" I asked.

29

Andrew thought for a moment about this question, which puzzled me since most kids our age and even younger know their address off the top of their heads.

"I suppose I live here," Andrew said. "Yes. Here."

"No. I mean, like, where in Redvale do you live? You don't go to the school, at least I don't think, do you? So I can only assume you are either homeschooled or live far away."

"You asked another question, Matt."

"You don't have to answer that one. Just answer the one from before–about where you live. Where do you live?"

"Here. I said that already. I live here. Please don't make me say it again. My turn. Have you ever wanted to get back at Ben for treating you so terribly?"

What kind of question was that? I thought to myself for a moment, trying to let both his answer and his question settle in my brain, but without success. I decided it best to just answer the question and keep the game going.

"I suppose I would. It would be nice if he got a taste of his own medicine, I guess."

"You should go home." Andrew said. "I think you need to get some ice on that eye. I'm sure your mother is going to be worried about you."

"What about our game? You don't want to finish?"

Andrew stared at me.

"No. We will play tomorrow."

"I don't think I'll be allowed to come here tomorrow after my mother sees…"

"We will play again tomorrow. I promise." Andrew said, sternly. "Goodbye, Matt."

He kept his eyes locked onto me, his lips tight. Without

arguing, I stood and left, making my way back to my house where my mother stood outside waiting for me.

———————

Just as expected my mother came up to the school in the morning, calmed down briefly from the evening before when she first witnessed my eye, but still in a strong rage. She yelled at the principal, whom she demanded to see immediately as she entered the administrative office. When they saw my face, the woman at the front desk could only assume what my mother was there for and did not want to stand between her and the principal. She got the tall, bald man, who then escorted my mother back to his office. I sat next to her in the small, stuffy room lined with diplomas and degrees as she pointed to my face, then to the school, then to him, all while raising her voice to just the right volume to be intimidating but not belligerent. The principal agreed that this should not have happened and swore to have my classes changed as soon as I told him who the boy was that hit me.

When I told him it was Ben, his face went pale.

The principal told us that there was some kind of accident and that Ben would not be in school for some time. When I asked, more out of a response that a well-thought-out question, all the principal would say was that he was walking home later in the evening last night and that something attacked him. The school was going to issue a warning to all parents to be sure their kids stay in after dark and to be cautious with where they go in Redvale until everything was figured out. I asked the principal if Ben would be okay and he said that Ben is alive, but had suffered some serious injuries–some that he would never recover from.

When I got up to leave the office, a police officer met me outside the door and asked if he was able to speak to me. The question was directed at my mother, seeing as how he would certainly need her permission first, but he stared right into my eyes as he said. His eyes read like a book. He thinks I had something to do with Ben's attack. He thinks I did it.

The officer sat me down in an old storage room that had been turned into a work room of some type by adding a small table and four chairs to it. I hadn't seen this room before and, if it wasn't for this specific moment, probably would've gone my entire middle school career without even knowing it was there. My mother sat down in the chair beside me, but the glare from the officer hinted to her that maybe it was best if she weren't there. She gave me a comforting pat on the shoulder and stepped outside the door, shutting it behind her to leave me alone with the cop.

"What's going on, son?" he asked me in almost a whisper.

"I don't know," I replied. "And I don't know what happened to Ben either! I really don't!"

"Can you tell me about your relationship with Ben? I know you two weren't exactly friends. Did he ever hurt you?"

I was stunned at the situation. I could feel my palms begin to sweat and I couldn't seem to keep my leg still. It bounced uncontrollably under the table.

"Hurt me how?" I asked the officer who was now holding a pen and paper, ready to write down my responses. "He was kind of a bully, but I'm telling you that I had nothing to do with anything! I really didn't! I swear!"

"Calm down, son," the officer said, peering at me over his clipboard. "Please don't make me say it again. Now tell me where you were yesterday after school, between three-thirty and seven PM."

"I was with Andrew."

"Is Andrew another student here at the school?"

"No."

"Relative?"

"No."

"How do you know Andrew?"

"I met him at the bridge."

The officer laid down his pen and clipboard and put both hands firmly on the table, his eyes piercing through me like I had said something wrong. He stood up, letting his legs push the chair out from under him and raise his voice, but restrained from yelling.

"If you don't want to start cooperating, son, we can take this to the station–and I don't think your mama is going to be too happy if we all have to go down to the station with you in handcuffs. Is that how you want this to play out?"

I shook my head. "No, sir."

The officer sat back down, scooting the chair up to the table with a loud scrape across the floor. He picked up his utensils again and nodded at me, never releasing me from his stare.

"I was walking through the woods after school when I had a really bad day. I was by this bridge and there was a boy named Andrew. We talked and I have seen him a few times now. He's short, looks younger than I am but says he is older, has brown hair and really blue eyes. Like, the bluest of eyes. I don't know his last name or where he lives. We only meet at the bridge. I've never been to his house or nothin' like that, I swear it. Yesterday, when we were talking, he asked about Ben and about my black eye. I left Andrew before seven, so maybe he did something to him."

"Does Andrew know Ben?" the policeman asked. "Have they met before?"

"No. Never, sir." I said back, quietly. "They haven't."

"Tell me exactly where this bridge is. We will go look into it later. Until then, I need you to stay away from Andrew and not go out exploring anymore–not until this is figured out. Understood?"

"Yes, sir." I said, nodding. "Can I ask one question, please?"

"Go ahead," the officer said, sitting back in his chair.

"What exactly happened to Ben?"

The cop sat forward, putting his elbows on the table.

"You genuinely don't know?"

"No, sir."

"He was beaten. Attacked. Somebody messed him up real bad. And whoever did it, whether it be you or Andrew or whomever, they're going to serve their time. This boy is barely holding on. He will never be the same. Ever. And I will personally see to it that justice is served here. Am I clear, son?"

"Yes, sir."

The officer went to the door and let my mother into the room. She looked to me with so many unspoken questions, of which I certainly had no answer to. The policeman explained to her that I needed to stay home and she agreed with him on that point. He repeated himself to be absolutely sure she understood that I was to go nowhere but school and she again tilted her head in agreement while gazing at me with the saddest of eyes. I stood from my chair and my mother took me home. I wasn't staying in school that day. I think we all thought it would be for the better.

———————————

I sat in my room, flipping through one of my old comic books, trying to forget the conversation that had happened only an hour prior. I wanted to forget about the officer. I wanted to forget about Ben. I wanted to forget the terrible look my mother gave me that showed me so much regret that I couldn't begin to understand. But most of all, I wanted to forget about Andrew. I wanted him to no longer exist; to be woken up from this dream and be back in the woods. I wanted to believe that the viper had bitten me and that this was nothing more than some messed up fever dream. I knew it wouldn't happen though. I knew I was only making things worse by lying to myself.

My concentration was broken by a tapping on the window.

When I turned my head to see what the source of the noise was, my throat plunged into my stomach as if I had swallowed a stone. Andrew was standing at my window, staring at me, not blinking, with those giant blue eyes. As I watched, he slowly knocked again, maintaining eye contact. I shut the door to my bedroom and opened the window enough to put my head out.

"What the hell did you do?" I said to him aggressively,

but hushed enough that my mother wouldn't be able to hear. "What did you do to Ben?"

"We never finished our game, remember?" Andrew replied. "Truths. We never finished. I wanted to finish."

"I don't care about your dumb game anymore! The police are pinning me on something I think you did! What did you do? Why?"

"I'll go first." Andrew said calmly. "Did you tell them about me?"

"What?" I sputtered. "What are you talking about?"

"Did you tell the policeman about me, Matt? It's my question. For Truths."

"I–I had to! What else was going to do? Let them take me to the station or even to jail or something? I don't want that! I didn't do this!" My voice was getting slightly louder as I tried to keep myself in check as to remain secretive about my guest in the window.

"They aren't going to find me, Matt. That was silly of you to talk about me to them. I can tell you don't like them. You don't like them any more than you liked Ben."

"I need to go. If they see me talking to you…"

"They won't. Don't worry. Your turn. Ask a question."

I thought for a moment before blurting out the only question I actually wanted an answer to.

"What are you, Andrew? Honestly."

Andrews lips curved up a little when he heard my question.

"Silly Matt. I'm your friend." His focus swiftly moved over my shoulder after the words left his mouth. "Close your window. Your mother is coming."

I turn to look towards the door. When my face goes back to

the window, Andrew is gone. I shut the window and latch it, just as my mother opens the door to my room.

"You okay, sweetie?" she asks me. "Do you want to talk about anything?"

"I'm okay, Mom. Thanks."

She smiled.

"Don't worry. We are going to figure this all out, okay?"

She went to shut the door, but my voice stopped her from doing so.

"Mom?" I asked. "You believe me, right?"

She paused.

"Sure, honey."

She closed my door and left me in silence. I knew she was lying. I heard the wind blowing strong outside of my window and I could see the trees from the woods off in the distance swaying. I needed to talk to Andrew and figure this all out. I needed them all to know it wasn't me. Andrew did this.

I head my mother gasp from the other room before the footsteps, heavy and fast, came towards my room. My door swung open with a force that almost pulled my mother to her knees as she came into my bedroom. I looked at her wildly with confusion.

"Sorry," she said trying to catch her breath. "Matthew, you need to see the television. Right now."

She led me into the living room where I could see the glow from the TV in the dark. On the screen I saw an image of a man in uniform with an American flag behind his head. There was an announcer, articulating his words with a sort of staccato, but I didn't have to listen to know what had happened. The banner above the picture told me everything I needed to hear. It was the officer who questioned me earlier that day. The banner above said his name and a declaration that he was now dead.

———————

If I thought the kids at school hated me before, I was quickly shown that it could be much worse. I was the plague. Everyone who knew my name, and even those who didn't, knew that I was a cursed young man. Or possibly a murderer. Or both. They knew that if I didn't like them or if I had any fraction of a reason, that they would end up injured, attacked…or dead. I had no idea what to do as I watched the crowd of kids part and push themselves against the lockers as I passed. They were horrified. The teachers felt the same way and refused to call on me, staying far away from my desk. I was not called into the office. I was not questioned by any police. I was ignored. And to be completely honest, I didn't mind it too much.

They never found who killed that police officer. They never found who attacked Ben. They couldn't prove that it was me and, for quite some time, they all left me alone. But it wasn't just the people at school. It was everyone. Every person I came in contact with in this small, chatty town knew who I was and knew what they believed I had done. My name was synonymous with death and before I even made it to high school, people were horrified of me. Even my own mother. I think that is what bothers me the most. My mother didn't want to hang out with me or discipline me or even speak to me unless she had to. I knew she thought the same thing as everyone else in this town. She thought there was something wrong with me—that I was sick or an omen or something. I tried to explain that it wasn't me an that it was Andrew, but she didn't believe me. I even offered to take her to the bridge, but she refused. She didn't want to go anywhere with me and, though she didn't admit it, I could tell it was because she honestly had convinced herself that I was this monster that the community had made me out to be. It all needed to stop. It needed to be brought to an end right now. I threw on my jacket and headed out towards the bridge yet again.

Andrew sat on the edge of the covered bridge, his back turned towards me, staring into the darkened tunnel. I stood directly behind him and waited for him to realize that I was there. Without turning, he spoke.

"Good evening, Matt," he said. "Have the police talked to you any more?"

"You know they haven't, Andrew."

"Good. That's very good," he replied.

"Your turn. Ask," I said, sternly. "Truths. It's your turn."

"I suppose it is," Andrew said, spinning slowly on his heel in a manner that made it seem almost as if he was levitating. Andrew's face appeared to be more pale, which only made the scar on his face protrude and flush with a light pink. "Are you enjoying your peace?"

"No!" I said back. "I'm not! People hate me! They are terrified of me and don't want anything to do with me!"

"That's a shame," Andrew said, his blue eyes meeting mine.

"My turn," I said. "Did you hurt Ben or the officer who

questioned me? Was that you? You have to tell the truth. It's the rules."

"I thought they were people that you didn't like, Matt. I thought you would be happy that they were gone."

"No!" I yelled. "No! No! No! This isn't what I wanted at all! I can't even speak to my own mother!"

"I'm sorry to hear that your mother is weighing on your mind."

I took pause for a second when I realized what I had just done. I should never had said her name. I should never have mentioned her at all.

"You stay away from her, Andrew! Stay away from her or I swear to God, I will finish you."

"Matt, you wouldn't do that. I'm your friend. Your only friend." His smile crept up his face, stretching far beyond what normal human lips could reach. I could hear his skin splitting in his mouth and he let out a childish laugh. "I'm your only friend, Matt! Your only friend! And I'll do what I want!"

I could feel my heart racing in my chest, fueled by the nightmarish appearance of Andrew, his mouth now the entire length of his face, his rotting, yellow and green teeth being licked by a blood-covered tongue. I stepped backwards then broke out into a run down the dirt path, Andrew cackling behind me.

When I made it to the house I screamed for my mother as loud as I could. I checked every room in the house looking for her, wanting her to be okay. She wasn't in the house. I looked out the window to see an empty driveway, meaning my mother was out. In a rage I ran out the front door and down the street, hoping to somehow, just maybe, find her coming home. I stopped at the end of the block and began to cry. She didn't come home that night.

In the morning, I didn't know what to do. I wanted to call the police, but I knew they wouldn't believe me. I couldn't tell them this horrifying childlike creature was attacking people and had my mother. I couldn't tell them anything that they would even humor. I skipped school and waited, praying to God and the universe and everything in between that my mother would come through the door. By noon, I gave up on waiting. I went into my mother's bedroom and, opening her bedside table drawer, wrapped my fingers around her six-shot revolver. I had never held her gun, or any gun for that matter. I didn't even know if it was loaded. I put it in my pocket, the metal bulging the denim of my jeans and the wooden handle sticking out at my hip. I made sure my shirt covered the whole weapon and decided to have one last talk with Andrew.

————————

Andrew was sitting on the dirt road, facing inwards towards the tunnel; right where he was standing the last time I came. I didn't say anything to him and he didn't turn. I stood behind him for what felt like an hour, but I knew was no more than just a few seconds. Andrew didn't move.

I pulled the gun from my pocket and held it as close to the back of Andrew's head as I could without touching it and pulled the trigger.

Nothing happened.

Andrew didn't turn around.

I pulled again.

Click. Nothing.

I could not get my hand to stop shaking. The revolver quaked in my hand, bouncing only an inch from Andrew's hair. I pulled the trigger one more time, this time with success.

The shot was loud and smoke blew out of the barrel. I felt the weapon leave my hand as it kicked and, when the smoke cleared, Andrew lay on his side, blood pouring from the back of his head which was now a mess of bone, skin and pink, leaking substances. I picked up the gun again and put it back in my pocket. I stared over Andrew's body, waiting for something–anything–to happen.

And it did.

Andrew's leg twitched within a moment of his laying there. Then his arm. In about a minute's time, Andrew pushed his body back to a sitting position. I stood, frozen in fear, trying to tell my brain to reach into my pocket and to take another shot. Andrew stood to his feet, still looking down the road and into the canopy of the bridge. His hand reached behind what was left of his head and his fingers explored the gaping hole I had put in it.

He took a step and shifted his body to face me. His face was pure white, not even affected by the bullet. His scar was almost red at this point. He brought his hand back down, shining in crimson as he wiggled those short, childish fingers in front of his face.

"Another scar, I suppose," he said. "Another scar from another friend. Such a shame."

"I'm not your friend!" I screamed at him. "I'll never be your friend! Leave me alone!"

"I know you're not my friend. Not anymore. And that's okay, Matt. It really is."

I stood, confused. I watched his hands slide into his pockets, and a grin draw upon Andrew's face.

"I found a new friend now," he said. "I found a brand new friend to play with, so I don't need to play with you anymore."

"Someone new?" I questioned. "What do you mean?"

"I found a new friend. He really needed someone to talk to. We've played Truths and you'll never believe what he told me, Matt."

"What did he tell you?" I asked, my voice trembling.

"He told me that he doesn't like you."

3

Showtime

When I die, I think they will bury me in a wooden box with a glass screen. It will have turning knobs and play music as you watch my body toss in my slumber. A small light will come from the transparent sheet and people will cheer or cry or whatever they choose while watching me die just as I lived–the man who attached himself forever to a television screen.

I say this all in jest, of course. I don't truly believe that I will make anyone go through the hassle of putting me in the ground while looking in at me from above. That seems wrong. And expensive. And not very kosher, if I say so myself. But I will admit to the fact that if it were anyone in the world to be buried in such a way, it would be me–the world's biggest fan of the wonderful world of television.

I think it all started when I was about three or four years old. I don't remember too much of it, as you could probably assume–that is a rather young age for one to recall specific details and what not. I do remember my mother consistently yelling for me to get away from the TV and that it was going to eventually ruin my brain if I sat in front of it for too long.

Silly old wives tale.

I never took the advice and could have only been more into

the channels if I had my forehead pressed to the glass, which I obviously didn't do. I knew every program that would come on every day and I knew exactly what time it would be on and what was going to happen in the next episode. I understood the basic algorithms to writing the shows and knew how the directors and producers created such wonderful stories. My parents grew to accept my addiction and allowed me to watch the TV as much as I wanted to, as long I helped them remember to tune in to their favorite shows, or fill them in on anything they would miss if they had to be at work or were out or whatever they did when they weren't in the living room with me.

When they finally came out with the VCR, I think that may have been the most money I had ever spent up to that point. I had saved every penny I had earned from random odd jobs and allowances and, within a few months of its release, I had one attached to the television in our home.

It changed the game for me.

I could now watch everything I wanted to and pick out what I watched by hand. Boxes and boxes of tapes all waiting to watched by none other than me. I would check out all the movies that I could and would spend even more hours in front of the screen, now that I controlled what it played.

When my parents passed away, I stayed in the home they had raised me in. I didn't have many bills to cover, so I only had to work part time (at the local video store, of course) to keep up my relatively happy lifestyle. I was alone, but I was content. I didn't need anyone else if I had my television.

I was happy.

I was fine.

───────────

I sat in my chair, the big brown one that used to be my father's. My elbows fell perfectly into the grooves on the arm-rests that I had put there like diamonds–built with pressure and time. I smiled as I turned on the box for the first time that morning. It was a Sunday which meant that I had no commit-ments whatsoever. My parents would have flipped if they had known that I stopped going to church after their passing, but I couldn't help it. I got nothing from the services and did noth-ing but take up space and a Bible.

The knock on the door came suddenly, which I responded to with a loud grunt, hoping that the person, whoever they were, didn't hear me. If they thought no one was home than maybe they would just leave. The lights were off in the house and I had muted the television right after the knock. If I sat here and didn't move, they would never know. Not to mention I wasn't expecting anyone, and frankly, I find it pretty rude for someone to show up at my front door announced. I have a phone–they could have at least called first. It was most likely some salesperson or one of the holy rollers or something. I didn't want more insurance and I didn't have a minute to talk about our Lord and Savior, Jesus Christ. I wanted to get back to my viewing.

There was silence. I waited to see if there would be any more signs of someone at the door, but nothing came. I sighed and turned the volume back up with the remote, which stayed lodged between my wrist and the arm of the chair.

Again came the knocking, but louder now.

Again I muted the television and waited.

I shook my head, trying to keep myself from growing angry with this person. I tried to remember that they were most likely just doing their job. Everybody needs a paycheck.

The silence returned and I made sure to give it that extra minute or so, just in case, before I pushed the button on the clicker.

As soon as the squishy plastic button was shoved down by my thumb, the visitor slammed on the door with what sounded more like a foot than a knocking fist.

It scared the devil out of me.

I jumped out of my chair, now cursing at the top of my lungs.

"I fucking swear, man, if you break my door, I'll have my foot so far up your ass that you'll be able to taste my toenails!"

I swung open the door to find nothing.

I peeked my head around into the front yard, waiting to see some kid running around the corner. As I surveyed the grounds from my doorframe, I became spooked at the lack of human presence on my stoop. There wasn't a person in sight. Not even across the street or outside any other houses. This person, this phantom of a salesman or kid or whatever they were, just disappeared.

I took one small step out to lean my head further, hoping to expand my view when I felt my foot hit something on the ground in front of me.

A box.

A package on a Sunday?

On the stoop was a small, cardboard cube with no name or

address written on it. I nudged it again with my foot, hoping to gauge the weight of the thing, as it moved with the pressure from my socked toes. It wasn't very heavy.

I gave one last look around, hoping this wasn't some trick or that someone would come to rob me as I bent down to pick up the box, which I had heard was becoming a new trend with crooks according to Channel 5 News. I hurriedly snatched the package and stood back up fast enough to give myself a case of the spins. Shaking it off, I stepped back into the house and placed the cardboard onto the loose, shaky coffee table in front of my viewing throne.

"What the hell are you?" I asked the box as if it would be able to respond. "I didn't order anything. I don't think I did at least."

I tried to peel the tape off with my nubby, chewed-down fingernails. It took a few minutes to get the corner pulled back but when I attempted to rip off the adhesive mess it tore up towards the side, forcing me to get up again to retrieve a butter knife from the kitchen.

Cheap-ass packing tape.

I slid the dull blade under the flap of the box and drew it forward, finally freeing the lid, allowing me to see the contents inside. Once I got through the crumpled up newspaper, which I lazily threw onto the ground beside me, I saw that there was a neatly fold T-shirt inside with some bright green lettering on it. Must be some promotional bullshit. Dammit. All this effort wasted for some gimmick for a company I am sure I never heard of before.

I pulled the shirt out and tossed it over my shoulder, revealing the postcard that lay underneath. The colors on it screamed at me in voices of neon pink, green, and yellow. How obnoxious.

Pinching it to pick it up, I lifted the card into the light of my table lamp that sat next to my chair.

> DEDICATED VIEWER!
> CONGRATULATIONS ON BEING
> SELECTED FOR THE CHANCE OF A LIFE-
> TIME!
>
> YOU ARE CORDIALLY INVITED TO PAR-
> TICIPATE IN OUR LIVE TELEVISION EVENT
> OF THE CENTURY!
>
> MONDAY, MAY NINTH, TWO-THOUSAND
> AND SIXTEEN
>
> PARKWAY STUDIOS
>
> NINE-THIRTY AM
>
> PLEASE WEAR THE ENCLOSED SHIRT
> UPON ARRIVAL

Was this some kind of joke? The television event of the century? This made it sound even more like a gimmick. Not to mention, the ninth was tomorrow. I chuckled, grabbing the shirt from my shoulder and holding it out in front of me.

> LUCKY CONTESTANT #5

The green lettering on the black shirt made my eyes hurt. Whoever designed this shirt did an absolutely horrible job, I thought. Not to mention, this would look horrible on the small screen, even with the nicest of televisions, high definition or not.

But how much fun would it be to be on TV?

The idea sat on my brain well after I folded the shirt up and put it back in its container. How funny it would be for someone like me, someone my size, to be competing in some event–assuming it was a physical challenge. The years had not been too kind on me and my viewing doesn't exactly burn calories to the extent that I would like it to. My multiple-XL frame most likely would not fit into any of the one-size-fits-all assumptions that the studio had probably sent as a shirt. Even if I wanted to go, I wouldn't even want to think about squeezing into the medium-husky default size that was lying in the box.

That would be embarrassing, to say the least.

My curiosity did get the best of me though.

I opened the flaps once more to see the shirt sitting folded as I left it. Observing the tag, I saw that the letters on it read: XXL.

How interesting.

They knew my size?

No. Lucky guess.

Had to be.

I grabbed my laptop from the table and turned it, telling myself I wasn't going to look up more information about the mystery package, but knew deep down that it was all I wanted to research. I don't often use the computer and, admittedly, am pretty poor at understanding it, but the internet came with the cable package and it would be a shameful waste not to put it to use every now and then.

I fumbled around the keys, trying to remember my password, typing in every variation of what I believed was correct until the jingle played and my home screen popped up. I surfed the web for a moment before finally making attempts to find any information about the event.

Nothing.

I was hitting nothing but dead ends. I searched forums of other people talking about contests, and maybe it was my lack of ability to use the internet properly, but I couldn't find a single thing about people getting random boxes in the mail or spontaneous invitations to television shows. I decided to look up the studio, which had been a real studio back twenty-some-odd years ago, apparently, but nothing relevant had been posted about it for quite some time. If I had to guess, I would have thought that it would have been renovated into something else by now.

Regardless, giving into my temptations, I pulled the address of the studio–just in case I decided to swing by some time, just to see if this place was a real studio or not. It was about an hour's drive from my house, so I didn't know when I would exactly be "in the area" to give it a peek, but I figured it wouldn't hurt to have it tucked away. I wrote the numbers onto a piece of scrap paper and placed it on top of the shirt before closing the box and returning to my viewing.

———————

I woke up the next morning to the sound of my alarm screeching in my ear. I rolled over on my lumpy mattress, kicking the blankets away so I could use my hands to support my body. I had fallen off the bed before and ever since had always habitually been frightened of it happening again.

I shoved myself up and slid my feet into my matted slippers that waited for me off to the bedside. I shuffled into the kitchen, poured a large bowl of cereal with no milk, and then sat on my chair, letting my body fall quietly into the grooves. There, in front of me, was the package, taunting me to open it up for one more look. I glanced at the clock on the wall, showing me that it was only seven twenty-five in the morning. If I wanted to go, I could still make it.

"Don't be stupid," I said out loud to myself.

I grabbed the remote, but couldn't help but to glance at the cardboard. What would it hurt to drive up there? It isn't like I had other plans for the day really. I didn't have to work at the video store until tomorrow. I would miss *Family Feud*, which would be a shame, but I would be home in time to catch the rerun, I'm sure.

"Fine," I said, letting the box know it had won. "Just to look, then right back home."

I grabbed the shirt, threw it on, put on some jeans that lay over the footboard of my bed, slid my feet back into my house slippers, and made my way out the door.

It was hot out. Even with the car windows rolled down in my beat-up old Chevy sedan my parents had left behind, I could feel the heat. It was at least eighty degrees, which most folks would have enjoyed, I'm sure, but when you live in the luxury of a permanently sixty-five degree house, you tend to notice these changes. I didn't like it one bit.

I sped through the traffic, which seemed light for this time of day. I had no complaints about it though; seeing as how it meant that I would be getting back home all the sooner.

I finally turned onto the winding road that led back to the location of the studio, surprised that there was no gate or anything to keep regular pedestrians–the viewing peasants like myself–off the property.

The building looked to be in better condition than I had expected. A lot of the time, when a building was abandoned, which this place definitely was by the lack of cars and simple "old" look it had going for it, you would see kids throwing rocks at windows or people leaving trash all over the place. This building, though certainly not in use, was still pretty clean. At least, the outside was.

I stepped out of my car and walked up to the door, noticing a piece of paper taped to the red-painted steel.

CONTESTANT ENTRANCE

"Well, no shit," I said, cracking a slight smile. "I guess this really is a thing."

I yanked the handle, pulling the heavy door which creaked on its hinges as it parted from its frame. The moaning of metal-on-metal echoed through the trees that surrounded the building. No light came out from the inside, however a smell of musk and age sure did. I shuffled my way into the building, still holding the door with the back of my heel.

"Hello?" I hollered in. "Am I in the right place? I have an invitation."

It wasn't until I said it out loud that I realized how stupid I sounded. I have an invitation. This whole damn thing was a hoax and I fell for it. I bet there was a camera hanging around here somewhere and they now have the image of pudgy me, wearing a dumb T-shirt, thinking I was about go get my big break. Way to go, assholes. You all got me–whoever you are.

I turned to leave when I heard feet moving from inside.

"Hello?" I said again, this time with a tinge of fear. "Anyone there?"

Nobody replied, but the sound of footsteps continued. I leaned in to listen, letting my foot slip from in front of the steel door, allowing it to slam shut. I jumped at the noise and stood in the dark for a second, awaiting an angry cursing from a janitor or possibly a homeless man–whoever was supplying the steps.

Still nothing came.

I stood, lowering the volume of my breathing, too frightened to move. I don't know why I couldn't turn and walk out the door and back into the light of the outside world, but I just couldn't. My feet were stuck to the hard concrete.

A light turned on down the hallway and I heard music. Cheery, dance-like, game show music. The kind you hear during the opening credits of a daytime program. With the light, I could see that the room I was standing in was large and empty. It must have been one of the backstage entrances, I thought. So strange.

I made my way towards the light with caution in every step. The music grew louder as I approached, bouncing off the walls and right to my face. As I inched my way through what turned out to be the side entrance of this studio, I saw the empty chairs where you would expect there to be a live audience. With the music blaring, it made everything seem even more off-putting than it already was.

Fuck this. I'm out.

I started back towards the door when I heard a voice call out to me.

"Lucky contestant number five!" it shouted. "You've made it! Come on down!"

I turned around to see the edge of the stage and seats still, but no one within eyeshot. Whoever this was must be upstage of my view. I peeked around to view the whole stage only to find it empty.

"Up here, son," the voice said again.

Among the rows of chairs sat a thin man, pale and dreary looking. He had on a green suit that was very obviously too large for his lanky frame. His brown hair was combed over neatly to the side.

When I was seven, I remember my mother making me go visit my Aunt Lacy. This was her sister who she was rather close with, but lived a few states over, so we only saw her on occasion. That year, Aunt Lacy died from stomach cancer. The disease ate away at all of the weight she had gained in her youth and left her as skin and bones. It made my mother so upset to see her like this.

This man looked like my Aunt Lacy before she died of cancer. Not the best image to see in what was previously believed to be an abandoned building, if I say so myself.

"Who are you?" I asked as the music lowered. "What is this?"

"Why it's a game show, silly!" the man replied. "You, being a man of such broad knowledge of television, should know that much, right? Tsk, tsk, tsk. You won't do well in the game if that is the level you'll be playing on."

"What game is this?" I asked him. "I've never seen this set before. I've never seen any show like this. I've seen everything local around here. I would recognize this set if it was ever on the air."

"We have a very small viewing population." the man said, never dropping his cheesy, too-big-for-his-face smile. His teeth were perfect. Huge and shiny white.

"I'm sorry. I think this was a mistake."

I turned around on my heel to make a run for the door, but am stopped by another man, who I know was not there when I walked onto the stage. This man was huge. Larger than most bouncers I had seen on the crime shows and bar makeover shows. He was probably around seven feet tall and easily three hundred pounds. He held his hand out to stop me, not saying a word.

"Nonsense!" said the happy man, adjusting his tie as he rose from the chair. "Come! Stay!"

The large behemoth nudged me towards the open stage where, on top of a dull carpet, there sat two chairs; one for a host and one for a guest, as told by the classic desk and side table. On each was a mug, the same color green as on my shirt, with steam rising from the opening. As I approached the guest chair I could see that it was brown. I could only assume it was coffee.

"Have a seat!" said Smiley, as he came down the stairs to join me on stage, his limbs twitching slightly like a cartoon man on crack. Now in the light I could see that his eyes were rather sunken into his head, making him appear even more sickly than I had originally believed him to be. His face twitched along with his body.

As he took his first step onto the stage, the music flared back up, and light took over the room. The man slid a microphone from his sleeve as a voice played over the music.

"Good evening ladies and gentlemen and welcome to another episode of *Shock! And! Save!* You supply 'em! We might just fry 'em! Here's your host, Johnny Thunderrrrr!"

A fake applause track roared over the music as it dimmed and Johnny Thunder, this decrepit man in the green suit, sank into the chair behind the desk, still grinning from ear to ear. The applause and music all faded until there was a silence in the studio.

"Good evening, ladies and gents, and welcome to another episode of *Shock and Save*–the only game where your knowledge can truly make all the difference. I'm Johnny Thunder, your host and today we are joined by Contestant Number Five. Wave hello to all the folks at home, Number Five!"

"I'm sorry. I need to go." I lifted my heavy self out of the chair and started off towards the side. The giant man shook his head and pointed to the chair. I turned to go towards the other side of the stage and there, to my surprise, was a man, just as large, but holding a baseball bat in one hand, slinging it over his shoulder. This man looked had a fairly large scar down his cheek and his shirt was slightly tighter than the other man's, showing off his bulging muscle.

"What the hell is this?" I yelled to Johnny Thunder. "I want to leave. Now!"

Johnny shook his head, still smiling. "But Contestant, the game has just begun. Come have a seat."

The fake applause track sounded off again as he gestured towards the chair and side table. It got louder as I approached them. When I sat, the crowd broke and there was hooting and even more cheering being screamed out of the speakers.

Johnny gestured to the empty chairs to quiet down, raising and lowering his hands before making eye contact with me.

"We are just so glad you could be here tonight," he told me.

"Please tell me where I am," I begged of him, trying to keep my cool. "I just want to go home."

"Why, son, you're on – "

"*SHOCK AND SAVE!*" yelled the loudspeakers, mimicking a crowd.

"I know that, but, I mean, what is this? Where are all the people? Where are the cameras? I really would like to go home." I thought about running for it, but I knew that those men on the side stages would not be hesitant to grab me–and sure as hell wouldn't have a hard time doing so.

"Should we explain the game to him, folks?" Johnny asked the chairs, who roared in return. "Sounds good to me! So, Contestant Number Five, the name of the game is *Shock and Save*. In this game you will be met with a series of quiz rounds. In each round you will be asked a question about today's television, of which we know you are quite the master of! When you answer correctly, you'll hear this sound!" A *ding-ding* noise sounded overhead. "But if you get the answer wrong, well then someone has to get the shock of a life time!"

"What do you mean the shock of a lifetime?" I asked, nervously.

The speakers cheered louder than before as Johnny looked out to them, then held his hand behind his ear, egging it to blast out more sound, as if he couldn't hear it.

"Should we show him, folks?" Johnny screamed at full volume, standing so quickly that I thought his frail body might just collapse. The noise was piercing as Johnny motioned to the wall behind me, which lifted, revealing four more chairs. In each chair sat another person, each with a shirt that said "LUCKY CONTESTANT #1" through "LUCKY CONTESTANT #4." They were all held to the chairs with thick straps, their mouths taped over, allowing only muffled screaming to be heard from their struggling bodies. My heart sank.

"Fuck this!" I yelled. "Fuck this and fuck you! This is sick!"

I jumped up as fast as I could and ran to the side where I was apprehended by the giant with no effort at all. I screamed for him to let me go and cursed at him, but he only dragged me back to the guest chair by the desk and Johnny Thunder.

"Oh, come on now, Number Five!" Johnny sang. "You're the lucky one! Would you rather be One, Two, Three, or Four right now? Because that can be arranged."

I looked over to the other contestants. All four were crying and trying to plead through the duct tape over their mouths. Johnny paid them no mind, keeping his gaze on me. I shook my head, silently.

"Good!" he continued. "As I was going to say, each contestant has a plate under their chair. Each plate is connected to a panel which my lovely co-host, Irene, will be in charge of."

I see a young woman step out from behind on of the curtains in a shimmering yellow dress. She looked just as sick and slender as Johnny, but with even less life in her eyes. She didn't smile. She stared off with her black-ringed eyes into nothing, as if she was on very serious drugs. Her hand reached up to a lever that hung from the wall.

"If Irene pulls that switch, a current of eee-lec-tricity will fire up from the floor, onto the plate, and send that contestant soaring! Or at least, trying to soar. They won't be leaving the chairs, I can assure you. Get the question right, however, and they will be able to go back home to their families! And that's how you play…"

Again the speaker had the crowd help.

"*SHOCK AND SAVE!*"

"This is disgusting," I said. "This has got to be a joke."

"Round one!" Johnny yelled, pulling a stack of cue cards from his pocket. "Are you ready?"

"Stop it. Listen to me! This isn't funny anymore. You got me! Ha-ha! Where are the cameras? The real host can come out now. You fooled me, okay? Damn. Please. Just stop!" I begged.

"What television show ran for ninety-eight episodes and featured Bob Denver as a bumbling, accident-prone crew man?"

"I–I don't know. I don't care. I want to go home now." I started tearing up. I could feel my stomach shivering as I sat in the chair. This wasn't funny anymore. I brought my feet up into the chair and put my chin on my knees, hugging my legs.

"I'm so sorry, Number Five. But that was not the correct answer! You know what that means!"

Johnny points to Irene who pulls down the lever. The sound

was a dull droning noise under the air that was pierced by the violent convulsions of Contestant #1 who hollered in pain through the tape. I watched her try to escape the chair, but the straps were too tight. Smoke started rising from the seat as her body went stiff, then crumpled over like a rag doll. The process took over a minute.

I threw up all over my own shoes.

"Alrighty, Number Five! That's one down! Let's see how you do with the rest, shall we?"

I shook my head as fast as I could. I wanted to speak, but no air was in my lungs to do so. The smell of burnt cloth and flesh was putrid.

"Here we go, Number Five!" Johnny continued. "Which family started in 1938 as a cartoon in the New Yorker?"

I peer over to Irene, whose hand was already on the lever again. Contestant Two was sobbing loudly. The answer came to me.

"*The Addams Family.*" I whispered, hoping that my answer would give some grace. Johnny Thunder looked down at his cue card, still smiling. Always smiling.

"That is…correct!" he shouted. The fake audience released a series of "boos" as the straps were released from Contestant Two who fell to the floor before running offstage. I heard the door slam behind her as she left.

The crowd quieted again at Johnny's command.

"Moving on," Johnny said. "Next question. Which television series holds the record for the most-watched episode of television ever?"

I cracked a small grin of hope, knowing that I had the answer right in the front of my mind.

"*M*A*S*H*." I said. "*M*A*S*H* does. One hundred and twenty-five million viewers." I moved my eyes from Johnny to Irene to see if her hand would drop the lever, even though I was positive that I was correct. The pause for Johnny's response felt like a lifetime.

"That is correct!" he hollered, grinning, but now with more of a menace. The crowd booed furiously. The straps on Contestant Three released and he ran off to the side, the sound of the door slamming followed his exit as well. Contestant Four stared at me. I saw his jeans had already been dampened with urine and it seemed as though his cheeks were full, which made me feel sick to my stomach. This man's life depended on my next answer.

"Are you ready for your next question?" Johnny asked.

I nodded.

"In the final episode of the series *Friends*, what was the famous last word to end the series?"

I thought for a moment. I could feel Contestant Four's eyes locked on me.

"Sure." I answered. "Chandler says 'sure' when asked if they should get coffee."

I saw Contestant Four squirm in his chair and I knew that had to have been the wrong answer. He struggled and tried his damnedest to break free of the straps, but it took only a few seconds for Johnny Thunder to announce that I was incorrect before Irene pulled the switch. It took a minute or so for him to die as well. He fought death the whole way down.

I held back my vomit and stood to my feet.

"That's it! It's over. The game is over. I want to go home now!"

Johnny stood, then guided me back into my chair.

"Not quite," he replied. "Have a seat."

Before I knew it, one of the giants was behind me, holding me down as another strapped my feet and arms to the guest chair. I hollered and pleaded, but it didn't seem to phase the giants or Johnny. Even when I kicked one of the huge men while he attempted to strap me, he didn't flinch. I was immobile.

"One. Last. Question." Johnny said, chuckling a bit. "Then you can go. Are you ready?"

"Let me go! You're a monster! A fucking monster!"

"The 116th episode of the popular series *Seinfeld* was called "The Soup Nazi" which portrayed a famous character played by Larry Thomas. What was the Soup Nazi's name on the show?"

I stopped struggling, knowing my fate if I didn't answer the question. I thought, but couldn't think of his name. What was it? Dammit. I had to know. I had to. Then it hit me.

"He didn't have a name!" I said loudly. "He was just The Soup Nazi!"

Johnny's smile faded as he nodded to the giants who then began to untie me. I remained in the chair and waited for Johnny to say something.

"That is correct," he muttered. "Well done."

No loud noises came from the speakers. I turned around to find that Irene and the giants on both sides of the stage were gone. Just as my head pivoted back, Johnny and the desk had all disappeared. The contestants, the furniture, the coffee–all of it had vanished. Then there was a single clapping sound coming from the audience.

I look out and, in the darkness, I could make out the image

of a young boy, smiling even larger than Johnny Thunder, clapping his hands at the conclusion of the show. I stood, turned and walked out the door.

The light and warmth had never felt so good. I reached into my pockets for my car keys when, while looking down, I bumped into something. Moving my chin up to see what I hit, I saw it was Johnny, but instead of a green suit, he was wearing grey and black coveralls. He was smiling.

"Oh, you don't think we actually let anyone go on *Shock And Save,* do you?"

I stumbled backwards, falling to the ground.

"How…but how can you…" I said, stuttering.

"Number Five, you should know better than anyone. Never believe anything you see on TV."

4

Dark

My grandfather was one of the strongest men I ever knew. Growing up, I looked up to him as a figure of what a man should be. He treated others with respect, loved with what seemed to be no conditions, and worked as hard as he could to provide for every single person that he cared about regardless of their relationship. He was the type that never forgot your birthday, made sure he attended every soccer game he could, and would sacrifice any of his own personal likings to be sure that you were able to get what you wanted. He never left the postman without a handshake and a sincere 'thank you' and never forgot to leave a few cold ones out for the trash men every Tuesday morning on the hot summer days. He was a good man. I thought the best of him. Until the night he died.

It was a chilly December afternoon and I had just gotten home from school when my mother told me that we needed to go see grandpa in the retirement home after his kidney started 'acting funky,' as he would often refer to it. He certainly didn't care much for his home and hated the limitations that came with it, but he knew that it was best for him and for the family. He was wise enough to understand that medical care was hard for people who loved him and even collectively, my mom and younger sister wouldn't be able to give him the round-the-clock service that his condition required.

I started the twelfth grade that year and expected that my final months in high school would be a breeze. I wasn't one to get stirred up into drama or trouble and had my small, tight-knit group of friends that I regularly hung out with. I thought that it would be as simple as going to class, heading back home, seeing my friends a few nights week, watching some TV, and doing my last few assignments before the school year ended and everyone started getting ready to move forward in life to the colleges of their choice, if they got in to any. I was lucky enough to get into my first choice at the University of Maryland, only a few hours from my home. I didn't worry too much about packing or prepping like the other students. I wouldn't ever be too far away from home if I needed anything at all. That evening in December was when I saw my grandfather for the last time. It was the last time that dreams of an easy life ever entered my mind.

We all got our coats on and jumped into my mom's minivan. I hated the drive into Grandpa's retirement community. It felt almost cult-ish to me, in a way. The community was in the middle of nowhere, somewhere out on the Eastern Shore of the state where the only ones who lived were the rednecks, old folks, and the bacteria that was sometimes thrown up by the Chesapeake Bay. It seemed like miles of cornfields and tobacco plants before we could even begin to see the long, empty road that led to the home. Most of the time I spent with my head pressed against the window, feeling the vibrations of the car as we rolled further into nothingness. After a small batch of trees that looked as if they were never fully in bloom, even in the warmest of weather, we would pull up into the often empty visitor parking lot, where my mother would habitually remind us not to veer off or get lost. This message was more for my seven-year-old sister than it was for me, but she always made sure that I was included in answering the question, "You got it?" I never had an issue with chiming in a "Yes ma'am" to this, but it was mostly because even though I hated the ride, I absolutely loved hanging out with my grandfather.

This trip, however, would be different. I could feel it. Not to mention, Mom would never spring a surprise visit to see him unless something was wrong. I was old enough to understand what this meeting probably was all about. I don't think my sister understood the weight of the situation yet, seeing as how she was still able to have a genuine smile on her face, while Mom and I, probably more obviously that we would have liked, forced out grins through tightly pursed lips. She took my sister's hand and walked us both up to the front sliding door.

A blast of cool air hit us as we entered the lobby and were greeted by one of the nurses at the front desk. I referred to people at the retirement home as nurses even though they probably weren't, but I figured it probably wouldn't hurt their feelings if they overheard me saying it, so I just stuck with it. I know a lot of the people there are only nine-dollar-an-hour employees, most likely trying to find something in a sort of medical field to build a resumé for college or, even better, someone who couldn't seem to find anything else to do with themselves for work in this little rinky-dink part of the state. I still to this day can't imagine that there is any real opportunity out there. Again, it's all old folks and rednecks. Neither of which are involved in big business. They waved us through without having to stop or sign in; they know who we are. The home only had maybe a dozen or so residents and if the parking lot is any indication of company, they didn't have all too many visitors. We turned down the hallway towards my grandfather's room and I could begin to feel a lump form in my throat that I couldn't swallow. My stomach turned hard and sunk down a bit, forcing my movement to slow. I suddenly didn't want to see my grandfather–not in the state that I imagined he was gong to be in.

My mom tapped quietly on the thin, hollow wooden door that sat ajar leading into my grandfather's tiny room. Though small, I will admit that they did a good job of keeping the place from being the dreary shit-hole it could have been. You hear some horror stories about retirement homes and how they can quickly resemble purgatory of some type, but this joint did all too well of making sure there were windows in each room, that there was open space, lots of places for pictures, art, what-have-you, and normal looking beds and furniture if the medical stuff wasn't a requirement to keep your ticker ticking. My grandfathers bed was, unfortunately, a medical bed though and there were, even more unfortunately, a whole system of tubes and wires coming out of him at this point.

He seemed to be asleep when we walked in so I asked my mother what exactly happened in a very hushed tone.

"Heart attack, kid," my grandfather said, trying to push out a chuckle over the tone of his heart monitor. "I was put here for my kidneys, but I'll be damned that my heart wants in on the action too."

"Dad, calm yourself," my mother said to him as she often did. This was almost like a tagline between her and her father. He would always be the spunky, spontaneous one, and she would always tell him to 'calm himself.' My grandfather smiled at this.

"Never listened to you before, Milly. Why would I listen now?"

I approached my grandfather with that forced smile and took his hand. It was cold and leathery. The toughness of his skin that had been there before seemed to have melted away and was now more smooth and boney. I could see the muscle loss that I never noticed before. When was the last time I saw my grandfather? I swore he was bigger than this before. All of these questions, I remember, rushed through my mind as his frail fingers wrapped around mine.

"Good to see you, kiddo," he said to me. "Been a while."

"I suppose it has," I replied, finally feeling more peaceful in hearing his voice. "How are you feeling?"

"I've been better, but I could be a lot worse." my grandfather joked. "They said that this one wasn't a big one. I refused to go to the hospital when they came to get me. Didn't need it."

"Which is exactly why we came, Dad," my mother chimed in. "Why didn't you go see a doctor?"

"What are they going to do, Milly? Tell me I'm old and I'm dying? Tell me to watch what I eat and to take my medicine? I'm far too far along to have anybody try to remind me of those things now. They should've spoken up twenty years ago. If my time is now, then it's now. Can't do much more about it."

"Don't say that, Grandpa," my little sister whimpered into my mother's thigh.

"Oh, little princess, don't you worry," my grandfather told her. "Everything is going to be just fine. Come give Gramps a hug!"

She grinned and made her way over to him, leaning up into the tall bed to put her arms around him. I saw him wince as she did this.

"Can we get you anything?" my mother asked him. "Is there anything you'd like?"

"Actually, yes, if you wouldn't mind," he replied. "Could you and the little one go find me something to eat, please?"

"Absolutely, Dad. Come on kids, let's..."

"Hold on, Milly," my grandfather interrupted. "Leave the boy. I want to have a man-to-man with him, if that's okay."

My mother's face was that of awe. In all this time, I don't think my grandfather had ever requested man-to-man time with anyone in our family and was certainly never one to hold any secrets from anyone. My mother simply nodded, trying to mask her confusion and curiosity, and took my sister by the hand once more.

"Sure thing. We will leave you men to chat," my mother said, gently guiding my sister out of the room. "We'll be back in five minutes, okay?"

"Sounds great." he said back. "Thank you."

My mother and sister left the room. I turned around just in time to see my grandfather shuffle himself up in his bed before grabbing my shirt and pulling me close.

"Listen to me, son, and listen well. You aren't safe. Not here, not anywhere, and you need to know it."

I gripped those thin, fragile hands not knowing whether I was trying to pull away or support his grip. I stared into his eyes for just a moment, which was more than enough to realize that he had tears forming like glass above his puffy eyelid.

"What are you talking about, Grandpa? Are you all right? Do you need the nurse?"

"No!" he said forcefully while trying to keep his volume low. "I need you to listen. A long time ago, long before you were born, there was an accident. I was working for the steel mills up in Pennsylvania right before I met your grandmother. A beam came down from the upper decks and hit me over the head. I blacked out and when I came to, there was nothing. It was dark. Everywhere there was black. All except one spot off in the distance. I walked towards that spot which seemed to be light coming up from the ground. A white light. Not like anything you'd see here. When I got close enough that I could reach out and put my hand in it, a shrieking noise, like metal on metal, rang out around me. I thought that I must be in the mill and that one of the machines must be running, but I knew better. There was no way that I was still at work and I remembered everything that had happened just moments before. I remembered looking up at the beam and I remember it slamming hard down across my nose. I felt my face, but there was no injury. When I looked back at the light there was a small boy, younger than you even. He was smiling at me. His eyes looked like a crystal lake in the morning. I knelt down in front of him, asking him what was going on. He didn't say a word. I saw that. I know his mouth never moved, but I heard him loud and clear. He told me that I was dead. That the accident I remembered was a true one and that it has shattered my face. He also told me that nobody at the mill had seen it happen and that I was still laying on the ground, broken. I asked him what was going on and I made a mistake, son. I made a terrible mistake."

"Grandpa, stop," I said, now trying to carefully pry his fingers from around my shirt. I could feel the jagged edges of his fingernails, as if he had tried to chew them off. He must have been gnawing at them for some time. "Let me call Mom and we can help you."

"You're not listening!" he said back to me, now a little louder. "We don't have a lot of time and please know that they will think I am crazy, but I know you will know the truth soon and I am trying to warn you before it comes. The boy and I made a deal."

"You're not making any sense," I said, horrified. "Let me go, Grandpa."

"There is a lot more to this world than you think. Those moments you think you're alone–you're not. Those moments in the peaceful dark when all is silent and there is nothing around but the sound of your own breathing, he is there. He doesn't come for us, son. He's already there. He's always been there. He's always watching. And now he is coming for you because I was stupid enough to make promises in my desperation."

"That isn't true. You're having another attack. We can help. Please!"

"This is no attack. I can feel it coming. It's cold. It's here. But it doesn't want me. It will take me all the same, but it isn't me that it wants. It wants you. The deal I made with the boy was for my son."

"Grandpa, you never had a son. You don't know what you're saying. You're losing your mind! Now let go!"

"I know I don't have a son, dammit!" he said, now raising his voice. "I only ever had your mother. But your mother had you. You must fill the void in the deal. You are going to be what they are after once I am gone and you need to stay safe. Stay in the light. He's in the shadows. He is there when there seems to be nothing at all. The dark isn't safe. It never has been. Not for many, many years. But now, oh God, now is the time and he won't show you any more mercy. He has waited for you for far too long."

The rate of his heart monitor picked up rhythm. Faster and faster the beeping grew as he spat more words out, followed by chunks of what I assumed was vomit and bile.

"Grandpa, I need to get a nurse!" I shouted now, hoping someone would come in to help him. "Nurse! Please! Someone help!"

"Stay in the light, kid!" he yelled at me, the yellow liquids dripping past his chin to his gown. "Stay in the light!"

His hands dropped along with his head, both smacking the railing of his bed with a loud crack like what you would expect if you dropped a plastic lunch tray–and made the same mess. He rolled back onto the bed just as his heart monitor rang out a single tone, blood gushing from the gaping wound in his head. His body gave one last jerk and he went to sleep. The nurses came rushing in, my mother in tow, yelling for my sister to stay in the hallway. They pushed me aside as I hugged my mother until my arms hurt. He didn't wake up.

———————————

The ride home was a silent one. We didn't stick around the home much after my grandfather passed, just enough for

Mom to fill out some paperwork before getting loud with one of the ladies at the front desk. I don't know what my mother was screaming about because she had asked me to take my sister and sit out front where they had a quaint little bench overlooking the small forest that surrounded the home. I couldn't make out words specifically, but I knew that voice, even when muffled by the thick exterior walls of the building. I could tell that they had said or done something to piss my mother off beyond a threshold that I had known to stay away from for quite some time. My mother is not an angry person, but if you push her the wrong way, she can unleash Hell.

She didn't say a word when she walked out under the awning where my sister and I sat. She marched herself to the van, knowing that I would be pulling my sister along behind me. I know that she didn't say anything to either of us until very late that evening when she came into my room to ask if I was okay. I told her that I was fine and though she smiled at me, this being the first I had seen her smile since we arrived at the home, I knew that she didn't believe me at all. She repeated her question and awaited a different answer.

I decided to try to tell my mother about what Grandpa had said to me. I told her about the pact he had made and the son he had promised and that I needed to stay in the light or else I would end up dead and all of the sorts. My mother just wiped a tear from her eye and patted my leg gently.

"Your grandfather was quite ill," she said trying to reassure me. "Please don't worry about anything that he said. I'm sure he didn't even know what he was talking about. I had a nice chat with the nurses today before we left about not being notified that his health was deteriorating. This only shows me that

I was just in saying what I said to them. I'm glad you told me. Don't take it to heart though. Obviously you are more than safe. You have nothing to worry about. He was too far gone to make any sense."

With a quick kiss on the forehead, my mom stood, turned and started towards the door of my room. With a forced smile, looking over her shoulder, she reached around the doorframe, flicking the light off in my bedroom as I lowered myself down under the sheets. I went to sleep.

I recall waking up to what felt like cold water being splashed over my body. The room was pitch black and I was surprised by the lack of light coming in from the street lights outside of my window. I sat up and immediately started to brush by clothes frantically, trying to figure out what had just been dumped on me. My clothes were shockingly dry. I noticed that there wasn't a lingering chill that hung like there would have been had I been doused. No drip of breeze. The rush came and went. I caught my breath and laughed to myself, now understanding that it must have been me waking up from some kind of nightmare. The fact that I was letting my grandfather's crazy, senile stories get under my skin was humorous enough to lull me back to comfort. I shifted my weight back and forth as I pulled the comforter up to my chin, stretching my legs and feet so that they both ran as two parallel lines, much like a ballet dancer's en pointe. I wiggled my toes, snagging them on something. I dropped my brow and felt around with my foot, attempting to feel out what was under the covers. As I rubbed my first and second toe together it became very clear. It was hair—long hair, like the top of somebody's head. I jumped up, hearing a thump of something large, like an animal the size of a dog hit the floor. Whatever it was landed on all fours and scurried under my bed as I began to push air out of my lungs, screaming as loud as my throat would allow. My mother came rushing into the room, filling every corner with light from the hallway.

"Mom!" I hollered. "There is something under my bed! Some kind of creature! I hit it with my foot and it ran under the bed!"

My mother waved for me to hop off the mattress and join her on the other side of the room, which I did without hesitation. She pointed to my baseball bat, an older Louisville Slugger, dark in color with lot of wood grains running along the rounded length of the club, which I picked up and handed to her as she neared the bed. I followed right behind her as she brought the bat into the air over her head. With a nodded signal, I reached down and pulled the skirt from the edge of the bed, making a hole for whatever was under there to run out of, only to meet its demise at my mothers best downward impression of David Ortiz at the plate.

But nothing came. Not a creature, not a sound, not any movement of any kind–there was nothing. Slowly, my mother bent down to peer under the bed and, upon realizing that there was nothing there, she promptly rose again, dropping the bat on the bed and giving me an ugly stare.

"I think those stories got you spooked," she joked with me. "Go back to bed." She gave me another kiss on the head, this time laughing under her breath before flicking the light off, leaving me standing in the dark, alone. I thought for a moment, swaying in place with my arms at my side. I knew what I felt. I knew what I heard. I was imagining it. Regardless of my grandfather's story, I didn't feel comfortable sleeping in the dark that night, so I shuffled over towards the door, reaching around, pressing my open palm around the wall, until I found the light switch. However, right before I flipped the tiny trigger up, I could have sworn I heard a giggle come from under my bed.

The next morning my mom cracked some joke about the "thing" that was under my bed. I chuckled and tried to brush it off, not letting it show that I got only an hour or so of sleep. She asked if I wanted to stay home from school that day, seeing as how the events of the morning before might have been a bit too much for me to take with me, reminding me that it would be okay for me to miss a day or two if I needed it for my "mental health." I declined the offer, grabbing my coat and backpack before heading out the door to start another Monday.

Third period was always my favorite. I had this wonderful teacher named Mr. Jackson who, according to any of the artistic kids in the school, was the coolest teacher you could have had for any of your classes. He was one of those old school hippie types–the kind of teacher that makes you wonder if he was simply grandfathered into his contract because you couldn't wrap your head around the fact that someone like him could get hired by the school board, even if it was to teach the arts. He mostly taught painting classes and elementary art to stuck-up, asshole kids who only took the course for an easy A, but my personal favorite of his was photography. I wouldn't say that I was a photographer by any means, but I admit that I really enjoyed spending my time developing the film and, by this, my twelfth grade year, I had made it to Photography 4, which both Mr. Jackson and I knew wasn't a real class, but rather an independent study course that allowed me to walk around the school for ninety minutes, looking for cool things to snap pictures of and develop them in the darkroom available in the back of his classroom.

During third period, I gathered all of my materials and pushed the sliding, ironically named, film container door–the kind that shielded the room from the fluorescent bulbs that shone blindingly over all the classrooms in the school–and got started with the beginning stages of developing my negatives.

If you have never developed film before, it is a pretty messy job. At least for high school kids. Unfortunately, most students didn't take care of the materials as well I did and it required a lot of washing out misplaced chemicals and having to be incredibly careful not to mix up the wrong solution in their improper containers–and also not to bump into the couples that would go into the darkroom to make out during Mr. Jackson's class, away from the eyes of the rest of the students. I filled up one of the large plastic bins with water and set it up across the small, black room, illuminated only by the dim red light above. I worked my way down to it, finally reaching the rinsing stage in my film development; excited about the photos I had taken of the garden built by some of the other seniors as a community project. It wasn't my normal subject of photography, but I was confident that some of them would turn out well and add some diversity to my portfolio that I had hoped to take with me to college.

I grabbed the negatives and dunked them into the water, slowly moving them around to wash off any unwanted chemicals before posting them up to dry. I jumped back and screamed when my hand hit something all too familiar.

Hair.

I looked down, my lower back hitting the sink behind me, to find my hand covered in wet, clumpy black hair. I used my other hand to quickly pull the mess out from in between my fingers when I heard bubbles gurgling from the wash bin. I inched over towards the bin, trembling, barely able to see that there was air rising to the surface of the water. A dark circular figure began to form inside the plastic tub underneath the bubbles. I couldn't make out any features of it, but I could feel my stomach drop, knowing all too well what it would be. I reached behind me to brace myself against the same sink I had slammed into just a second ago as the face of a little boy elevated over the lip of the bin, dripping water from his thick dark hair. Just as my grandfather had told me, his eyes shined like blue diamonds, even in the red hue of the room. He began to giggle, the same innocent and horrifying noise I had heard from my bedroom, as I ran to the spinning door, pushing through, and spilling my body out across the hard tile floor of the classroom, inviting the students to erupt in laughter. Without a word, I grabbed my bag and ran from the room, Mr. Jackson following close behind me.

My mom had me see a therapist later that week. She assumed that my grandfather's death had affected me in some negative way and was now playing tricks on my mind that she wanted to just have someone take a look at so it doesn't get any worse. I can't say that she was entirely wrong. His death had affected me. For the next two years I would see this boy, this pale young man, giggling at me in the dark. I learned to stay in the light and how to avoid any situation where I would not be able to see the world in front of me. I carried flashlights with me everywhere I went, fearful that the power in some building might go out, leaving me vulnerable to this boy and his wishes. The fear grew to a point where I avoided going inside altogether, except for buildings that had large glass windows that I could be assured would maintain light from the outside. I slept in my room with multiple lights, each battery powered, all installed at various times, leaving me with the security that there would never be a moment where they would all die out.

All of that changed when my mother brought me here.

Here it is better. Here they don't turn off the lights and have promised me that they have the generators to back the power up if a storm were to pass over. The white walls bring out the light and keep every corner of the ten by ten room shining, refraining from darkness. It is safe here. I never have to leave. I can sleep soundly, without worry of the little boy and his sinister motives. It is quiet and peaceful. They have told me that I can stay committed as long as I need to–and I never plan to leave.

5

The Graveyard Shift

We moved into the house shortly after I lost my job. It wasn't by any means a move we wanted to make and, truthfully, this was sort of a forced hand. My wife, Stacey, would smile and tell me that it would all be okay and not to worry about it–that we could make this new house our home and, when we get everything sorted out, that we could possibly move into an even better house than the three-bedroom townhouse that we had just moved out of. She was good to me, my wife–a woman stronger than I, even in the toughest of times.

My daughter, Lily, didn't take it as well as my wife. She is young and I don't think she could understand why we had to move away from her friends and the neighborhood where she grew up. I don't think she would've gotten the whole concept that Daddy's plant had shut down and, until Daddy could find a new company that paid even close to the same amount, that we would certainly have to downgrade. A lot.

I consider us rather lucky that Stacey's mother, who unfortunately passed away just a year before, had left us this property. The house on the land was pretty terrible, but livable for the tight spot we found ourselves in. We had initially tried to sell it, but couldn't find any buyers, not with it being out in the middle of nowhere and not with the condition of the house being what some might call more than just a fixer-upper. However, when all is said and done, it was the only thing that kept us from being out on the streets, so who am I to complain? We had a roof over our heads and running water. We had electricity and, with the money we got from selling our old house, which wasn't much but definitely a big help in the grand scheme of things, we would be able to have the power on for at least six months or more. We hoped that that would be enough time for me to get a new paycheck. We had already seen three months of no luck.

The first time my family and I stepped into the house as "our new home," it was a humbling experience. I had just had the power turned on the day before and as we flicked the lights on in the tiny foyer, you could see some creepy-crawlies dive out and under the furniture. This place needed a lot of love and a whole lot of elbow grease. I helped my daughter get her stuff to her new room–one of only two in the house. We gave her the room at the end of the hall, that way our room would sit between the stairs and her doorway. We did this in the old house and it was more so of a habit than anything, much like how I always slept on the side of the bed that was closest to the door in our bedroom. It was a protection thing.

We got my daughter's room set up first, putting her bed back together and getting some of her important toys and books into the room before we even got started setting up anything of our own. The first night, my wife and I slept on the mattress on the floor while the pieces of our bed lay strewn out across our would-be bedroom. The nights were chilly, as we tried to preserve the heat the best we could, but my Lily had many blankets on her bed and was able to stay warm. We wanted her to be as comfortable as possible. We knew this whole ordeal would be hard for her and we felt terrible about it all.

A few weeks went by and things started looking up, at least in the house. We were able to clean and dust until the house was sort of presentable. We got all of our old furniture in and my wife took the time to hang photos and made this ugly situation something just a little more pleasing. I searched every single day for a new job, applying online and going into shops and factories and dropping off paper applications before setting up interviews. That moment I got the phone call that let me know I had been accepted for a position doing warehouse logistics for a major shipping company was one of the happiest I had had in quite some time. My wife and I both cried after I hung up the phone, and though the position would involve almost an hour and half commute one way across the Bay Bridge towards the mainland, I would be making money similar to what I was making before. We could finally start the countdown to getting our lives back together. We could finally start thinking about taking back everything we had before and getting out of the sticks. But that countdown was a long one and we had a while to go before we could even start looking for a new house again. This place would be home for at least another year or two until we could build back up our savings, our credit, and be able to start over for, hopefully, the last time.

My first day on the job came quick and after a few trips into the office for HR purposes and drug screening and all of that jazz, I was finally able to start working my regular forty hours a week, unless overtime was an option, in which case I would never say no. My shifts would start pretty late at night and end early in the morning, which was great for a lot of the young bucks I worked with, boys in their twenties who decided not to go to college but straight into the workforce, but for someone with a family and a rather lengthy commute, I wouldn't call the hours preferred. But I reminded myself regularly that I was just happy to be working, that I had officially survived unemployment.

The shifts started around eleven in the evening and would end no earlier than seven in the morning. I drank a lot of coffee between those hours and though the job was considered logistics, there was still a lot of loading and unloading that I had to take care of. I spent much of my time helping to get the boxes off the trucks and onto the proper pallets to be shipped out to wherever the next driver would be taking it. Over these nights I would miss my wife and my daughter and wonder if they were okay. I would text my wife or leave her messages, even though she was certainly sleeping, just to say "I love you" or let her know I was thinking of her. Though it wasn't exactly what I had always dreamed of, I was happy.

But then things started to get a little...interesting.

I started out my work night like any other I had in the past few months. I clock in, grab a cup of coffee from the break room, look over some spread sheets to see what would be coming in that night and find out if there were any trucks that would be coming in later than expected. All seemed to be looking per the usual for the evening. Midnight came and went and, as I normally do, I sent my wife a quick text to let her know she was on my mind. I started back to work when my phone started to ring in my pocket. It frightened me at first, seeing as how I never get calls this late and when I looked down to my screen, I see that it is my wife. Thinking maybe she was trying to be sweet or maybe was still awake and wanting to say goodnight, I picked up with no urgency.

"Hey, sweet pea," I said into the phone. "Everything okay?"

I waited for a response, but nothing was said. Just silence drifted on the other end of the line.

"Sweetie? Are you there?" I said, this time just slightly louder, thinking maybe Stacey hadn't heard me the first time. Still nothing.

I gave it a few seconds then hung up the phone. I called her cell back and she picked up after a few rings, sounding incredibly tired and groggy.

"Hey, honey," she said. "Is everything all right?"

I laughed a little bit, surprised by her reaction, finding it adorable.

"Everything is fine, dear," I replied. "I was calling you back. You don't remember calling me at all, do you?" I chuckled a bit as I spoke, imagining her confusion.

"I never called you," Stacey said back to me.

"I think you sleep-called me or something. I definitely just received a silent phone call from you. I can send you a screen shot if you don't believe me. It's okay. I think it's cute."

Stacey made a humph noise before replying.

"That's so strange. My phone was on the dresser. I would have had to get up to call you and I was fast asleep. I don't remember it all. Do I normally sleep walk?"

"Not that I have ever noticed," I replied. "Did you have tea before bed or something? Sometimes your tea makes you a little goofy."

"No. No tea. Either way, I'm sorry, hon. I'll let you get back to work. I'll see you in the morning. I'm going to go back to bed."

We said our quick goodbyes and I got off the phone, putting it back in my pocket, thinking of how strange it was that Stacey would sleep walk–or even stranger, sleep dial me. Regardless, the night was busy and I had much to do so I got back to it, finishing my shift about half an hour later than expected, getting myself those few minutes of overtime I so desperately loved seeing on my paycheck.

I chatted with Stacey about the call when I got home that morning, and we just shrugged it off. She showed me where her phone was and we both simply let it fall under the "stranger things have happened" file of our brains before going on with our regular day. I slept, she did some house-work and saw that Lily got to and from school. I got up around the time my daughter got home and we sat downstairs, enjoy-ing a movie before it was time to put her to bed at eight o'clock. I walked her to her room and, after she got into her pajamas, I asked if she wanted me to tell her a story. She said that she didn't need a story, but wanted to know who the boy was that walked into Mommy's room last night. My gut turned to stone and I asked her what she was talking about.

"Last night I couldn't sleep and I thought I saw a little boy walk into Mommy's room. He didn't say anything to me or bother me. I wanted to say hi to him. I even waved, but he didn't notice me, I don't think. He just walked into Mommy's room and I didn't see him any more after that."

I told her that I thought it was all a bad dream and that maybe she shouldn't be up watching movies so late at night. She let out a little cry and told me that she liked her movies. I hugged her and told her to try to sleep and not to worry, even though I could feel my heart pulsing in my chest, stricken with a not-so-subtle fear. Lily gave me a kiss on the cheek and threw herself under the covers just as I exited her room.

I mentioned to Stacey what Lily had said and I could tell that it was a bad idea. Stacey looked terrified, which I should have expected seeing as how this was the woman who would cover her eyes at some of Lily's "spookier" animated shows. I told my wife that it was just a bad dream that Lily must have had and not to let it bother her. I even joked with her, telling her that she could sleep with the lights on if it really bugged her that much. She smacked my arm and told me that she didn't need to leave any lights on and that I needed to start getting ready for work so that I wouldn't be late. I gave her a kiss on the forehead and went upstairs to change before heading out the door and along my way across the bridge.

As normal, I texted my wife around one in the morning, but this time jokingly added a little line asking if she had seen anything creepy in the house. I figured she wouldn't see it until early in the morning, unless she had another sleepwalking incident. My phone sat in my pocket for about thirty seconds before I felt it buzz.

A text message.

I turned on my phone, looking at the banner that flashes across the screen, allowing me to preview that message before I unlock the phone. All it said was: "Yes."

Without any hesitation, I called Stacey, who again picked up sounding groggy. I asked her about the message which she denied.

"Check your phone, Stacey. I'm telling you, you texted me

'yes' when I asked you if there was anything creepy going on in the house."

She went silent for a moment before I heard her mumble "What the hell?" her mouth far away from the phone.

"Stacey, is everything okay?"

"Everything on my phone is deleted." she said. "Like, all of it. Contacts, messages, images. Everything is gone except for one picture of Lily. I don't like this. It's not funny anymore."

"I'm sure it is just a glitch, dear." I responded, trying to calm her down. "It's just a bug in the system or something. We can take it to the store in the morning and see if they can recover everything for you, okay? But just to be sure, you didn't send me any text messages at all? You're positive?"

"I would tell you if I did. I don't like this. I really don't like this."

"It's okay, dear, just..."

"I'm scared, baby."

Letting out a little sigh, trying to think of a different solution, I offered up the only thing I could think of that would possibly help.

"Do you want me to play sick? I can come home if you really need me to."

"No," Stacey replied. "Don't do that. It'll be fine I'm sure. I'll just turn on a movie or something; keep myself distracted."

"That's my girl," I said. "Don't worry. I'm sure it is all just a few spooky coincidences, that's all. I'll see you in the morning. Love you."

"Love you, too."

I hung up the phone and couldn't get the idea of a young boy in my house out of my head for the rest of the evening, even though I knew just how crazy it all sounded. The drive home seemed longer than normal, as I was anxious to get back to my girls.

I came home to the two of them asleep on the couch, Lily late for school. I was a little disappointed, but I was just happy to be home with them. I let them both sleep in and called Lily's school to let them know that she would be out today because she wasn't feeling well. Stacey apologized over and over again when she woke up, but I assured her that it was okay and that I was even a little happy to get an extra day with the both of them. We all went out into town and had Stacey's phone looked at, but unfortunately they said they couldn't recover anything from the card. It was such a strange occurrence, and I asked why that one picture, the picture of Lily, had stayed on. The young man behind the counter folded his lip and shook his head, telling me that he had absolutely no idea and that he was sorry he couldn't give me more answers. I told Stacey on the ride home that she could just copy all of the contacts out of my phone and if it happened again, that we could look into getting her a new one.

Once we got home, we had dinner and it was about time, as usual, for Lily to head up to bed. I went with her, this time with the reason of asking her a few questions.

"Hey sweetie?" I started as she tucked her feet under the blanket.

"Yes, Daddy?" she said, sleepily.

"Did you happen to see the boy last night? The one that went into Mommy's room? Did he come back?"

"Mhmm." she replied, quietly, shutting her eyes.

"He did?" I said, shocked. "Did he say anything to you this time or maybe talk to you about anything?"

I couldn't believe I was asking my four-year-old daughter about a figment of her imagination or a dream or something. Even worse, I couldn't believe that I was taking these answers seriously.

"He told me that he wanted to play a game with Mommy."

"What kind of game, sweetie?" I asked, this whole conversation making my stomach start to turn.

"He said he wants to play hide-and-seek. He said that Mommy is going to hide first, and then it's going to be my turn to hide. I said I didn't really want to play, but he just smiled and walked into Mommy's room. Then Mommy woke up and came in here, so we went downstairs to watch TV instead. We watched the princess again, Daddy. I like that movie."

"Did you tell Mommy about the boy?" I asked more forcefully than I probably should have. "Did you tell Mommy that the boy was going in her room?"

"N,." she said to me. "I thought she would know since she woke up as soon as he walked in. Her phone was buzzing and ringing too, so I thought she would have seen him."

"You're sure you weren't asleep, Lily? None of this was a dream?"

"No, Daddy," she replied. "I didn't sleep until we went downstairs on the couch. I promise. Are you mad at me?"

I could see small tears start to form in my daughter's eyes, so I quickly reassured her that I wasn't at mad at her and that I was very happy that she told me the truth. I asked her if she was going to stay awake all night again today and she said that she wasn't sure. I told her that if she sees the boy again, that

I want her to go wake up Mommy and have Mommy call me. She promised me that she would. I kissed her goodnight and finished tucking her in. I decided not to tell Stacey about this conversation and hoped that everything would be ok while I went to work. In a few hours I was back across the bridge, starting my shift.

I was certainly grateful to not have the kind of boss who lurked over my shoulder, seeing as how I checked my phone every few minutes to see if I had any calls or texts coming in. Nothing. Three in the morning rolled around and I still hadn't heard anything from my wife or my daughter so I could only imagine that things were okay. Suddenly there was an announcement overhead through the speakers, letting me know that I had a call waiting for me in the main warehouse office. I ran as fast as I could through the building, finally slamming the door behind me before taking the call.

"Stacey! Is everything okay? Stacey!" I yelled into the phone without thinking.

"Daddy, it's Lily," said a small voice on the other end of the line. "Why are you screaming?"

"Lily, baby! Where's Mommy? How did you get this number? Is everything okay?" I couldn't figure out why my daughter would be calling me at three o'clock in the morning, but I had a million different possible hypothetical emergencies that could be going on back at home.

"Mommy is playing the game with the boy," Lily said. "And this is the number you left on the fridge in case of an emergency, so I called because you told me to have Mommy call you when I saw the boy, but she can't call you 'cause she's playing right now."

"Lily. Listen to me, sweetie," I said, trying to remain calm. "I need you to give the phone to Mommy right now, okay?"

"I can't," Lily said, matter-of-factly. "She is playing with the boy and she isn't here anymore. She got up and left with him. She followed him out the front door."

"Out the front door?" I said, louder. "Lily, where is your mother? I need to speak with her right now!"

"She left with the blue-eyed boy, Daddy. They are off to play hide-and-seek. He said he would be back to play with me later, but I told him I wanted to ask my Daddy first."

"Lily, stay in the house, lock the door, and wait for me to get home!" I shouted. "Do you understand me? Stay in the house!"

Lily agreed as I hung up the phone, crashing it hard onto the desk. I ran to my boss, told him I had an emergency and needed to go home. What normally takes ninety minutes took about seventy as I tore down US-50, praying there wouldn't be any police officers to pull me over this early in the morning. I called the police to have someone check the house, but by the time they got there and had searched, I was pulling up the driveway. Lily stood with an officer, wrapped in a blanket like a trauma survivor.

"I told them they weren't allowed in, Daddy. Just like you said," she said, running up to me.

"It's okay. They're police officers. You know police officers are good guys. Now where is Mommy?"

Lily didn't say a word. I repeated my question to her but she just pointed out to the woods behind the house where I was able to see flashlights circling around. I turned to the police officer behind my daughter and asked if they knew anything about where my wife was and they all assured me that they were searching for her. There was no sign of struggle or forced entry and it seemed as if my wife had just gotten up and left. I ran through the entire house, but found nothing of my wife. Everything that belonged to her was untouched. The officers were right. Not a trace of anything suspicious. Just no wife.

Once the police had gone, promising to be back with the dogs when the sun came up, I sat with my daughter on the couch and asked her to tell me everything that happened. She said the blue-eyed boy had come into her room and placed his finger over her lips. She said that he said that he and Mommy were going to go into the woods to play hide-and-seek and that, if she was good and quiet, he would come back and play with her too. She said she watched Stacey head down the stairs with the boy and she heard the front door open. She watched Stacey walk towards the woods for a moment before calling me. Shortly after, the police showed up, followed by me.

We never found Stacey. The dogs searched high and low and so did many wonderful townsfolk that none of us had ever met. Lily and I did many news interviews, and talked to lots of reporters, but in time, everything went back to normal. People forgot, except Lily and I, and the police said they had done all they could. They think that Stacey must have run off, but I knew that wasn't the case. I tried to convince them to keep searching the woods, but they said they could find nothing.

A year later, I packed up everything and moved Lily and myself back in towards the mainland, closer to my job. It was terrible having to shift around hours and struggle through schedules, but the two of us finally got a routine down that worked, even without Stacey. It breaks my heart knowing that she might be out there somewhere, but I have no way of knowing where she is. Lily doesn't understand it all yet and I don't know how I am going to have to explain it all to her: that there couldn't have been some little boy and he couldn't have led her into the woods. She won't believe me when I say it was all a dream.

However, as of yesterday, I don't think I believe it was a dream either.

I woke up in the middle of the night to a bump down the hall. As I looked up, I saw my daughter, slowly walking towards the stairs past my bedroom door. I stepped out and grabbed her and she looked at me as if I had awoken her from a trance. I ask her what in the world she was doing and she told me all she could remember was the boy coming back.

And telling her it was her turn to play.

6

Drip

I walked towards Mr. Samuels' room with a syringe of calorie mush that I intended to squeeze directly into his stomach. This was the second and final time I had to do it for the day, seeing as how he was on a pretty regular schedule of it and, though he was pretty frail at this point, he essentially still only got two meals every twenty-four hours. They were heavy meals, though.

The way he had to take his food was rather disgusting, especially if you weren't used to seeing this kind of thing. There was a direct line, a tube, if you will, running from his stomach through his skin which had a cap that I could place the syringe into. Once the syringe was in place I would be able to slowly squeeze the yellow gobby mess into his abdomen, allowing him to not starve to death, seeing as how feeding himself was no longer an option. He hadn't fed himself in months. Not since the accident. Mr. Samuels, the bastard that he was, relied on the doctors and nurses to keep him alive. Along with the aid of the morphine drip, calorie intake, breathing apparatus, and other various tools. It was a waste of medical funding if you ask me.

I had been at this job now for about six years and, to be perfectly honest, it has never really gotten any easier. Not for one second.

That isn't to say that we don't have lighter days. These blessings come when we don't have people coming through the ER with some life-threatening shit–a spike through the head (which yes, I have seen), a gunshot wound through the chest, a suicide failure, or a child with no hope left. Those were the worst. There was nothing I hated seeing more than a little boy or girl who has been in and out of here more times than any human could ever deserve receiving painful treatments for diseases we don't have cures for and, more or less, are just waiting to die before they even see their tenth birthday. When I was just starting out, I spent many, many nights in the on call rooms crying my eyes out, thinking about what it would be like if that child getting the chemotherapy was my baby girl, only seven years old. Those poor families. Those poor, poor kids.

It never gets easier.

Never.

But then there are people like Mr. Samuels. He is the type who could rot in that bed…or on the floor for all I could care. One of the hardest things to stay true to as a nurse, in my experience, is that you have to treat each and every person without any sort of bias, no matter who or what they are. They are a life and it is your job to keep them alive. Period. End of conversation. Even if you don't think they deserve it.

Like Mr. Samuels.

This distaste for Mr. Samuels is shared by many if not all of the care staff here at the hospital. It is in no way just my own personal opinion. This man deserved to die when that pickup truck smashed in the drivers side door of his little sedan. He deserved to be pinned between the grill of the offender (who admittedly was at fault for running that red light) and the rubber of his center console. I think we all would have loved to see him slammed so hard in his seat that they would have buried him with a Ford logo permanently pressed into his forehead. But he survived. Unfortunately.

Mr. Samuels killed about a dozen little girls. He was Jeremiah Samuels, or what the media referred to as the Smoking Phantom after one of the parents claimed that the little girl's room smelled of stale cigarettes the day she went missing. I find it interesting because from what we can tell, Mr. Samuels never smoked. At least not recently.

Mr. Samuels was a sick, disgusting, vile human being.

He was left unconscious, thrown into a serious coma as soon as his vehicle was struck. I'm sure it did plenty of mental damage. For all we know, Mr. Samuels isn't really even there anymore–not in his head or able to comprehend the world at all. But we don't know for sure.

One of the police officers who surveyed the scene after the fact found Mr. Samuels' wallet in the front seat of the wreck. They used the ID, which was, in fact, correct, to go back to his house. Upon entering, they found a terrifying display of inhumanity beyond what they could've imagined.

The furniture was draped in skin, dried out and stretch like a fine leather, but cracked–obviously showing Mr. Samuels' less-than-professional tanning abilities. There were tiny bones in candy dishes and inside fishbowls where he kept many beautiful orange goldfish. The home smelled of rot and decay. The rest of the bodies were found later that week under the floorboards of the dining room, laid out in perfect little rows. There were parts of thirteen little girls in that house. Thirteen little girls who had been missing for months. Thirteen little girls that the town had searched high and low for, but to no avail. Thirteen little girls who could finally go back to their families to be buried like decent human beings.

But their murderer lived. Only barely, but he was alive nonetheless. And it was my job to make sure he stays that way.

———————————

The evening was chilly, but clear. I liked having the night shifts at the hospital if I could get them, that way I could be home before my daughter goes off to school and I could tuck her in if he actually went to bed on time. I know my husband often let her stay up after I left the house. He saw it as their little father-daughter bonding time. I always give him shit about how she is going to be grumpy at school when he does that, but I actually don't mind it too much. It is cute in a way, I suppose.

The night shift had a lot to offer. The rooms were often much more quiet and, besides the occasional scream-inducing injuries rushing in through the ER, it wasn't too bad if you could tolerate the hours. In my position, it involved mostly just checking in on patients and caring for the folks who needed my attention.

But that first time I saw him was a night that I don't think I could ever forget.

I specifically recall walking towards trauma where Mr. Samuels was kept. The halls were silent. I paused for a minute to take it in and tried my hardest to find any slight beeps or buzzes from the machines, but was happily unsuccessful. To be able to absorb the moment, I found a tight wooden bench up against one of the walls and had a seat.

No more than fifteen seconds had passed when I looked up to see this child, a boy, around my daughter's age, maybe a bit older, standing at the edge of the hallway. He looked tired and worn and his clothes seemed more ragged than I would have expected. I would be lying if I said that it didn't make me jump–maybe even let out an audible gasp.

The boy stood and stared at me from down the hall, pale as a ghost, but with blue eyes that shone like crystals, even from fifty feet away.

I laughed for a second to myself, understanding now how silly I must have looked to this boy, jumping like I did. I stood to my feet and made my way over to him. He didn't move a muscle.

This kid must have been one of the leftover kids from visiting hours. This wouldn't be the first time that a child has fallen asleep in the room while visiting grandma or grandpa, only to wake up well after the time they should have been gone. He is certainly young for such a situation–one could have only imagined that his parents would have been worried–but it was not my place to judge. I didn't know this kid's story. I didn't know if he had parents or a grandparent or why he was here. He very well could be a lost patient from the sixth floor, where many of the other children are, who happened to prefer his outdated attire to the standard hospital gown. All I knew was that he definitely was not supposed to be in this hallway and with me being the only one around, I should take him back to where he belongs.

"Hey, little guy," I said to him, smiling and dropping to one knee as I got close. "You lost?"

The boy shook his head and grinned eerily. I waited for him to speak, but he didn't seem as though he had any intent to, so I asked him again.

"Are you lost, bud? Can I help you find someone?"

He shook his head. Silent.

"Okay, well, I am going to need you to come with me, please. We should get you downstairs before someone else sees you. You definitely shouldn't be on this level. There are a lot of sick people here and we don't want you to get sick or…"

"Or die."

I didn't know how to respond to his statement. It sent chills through me hearing this child talk so casually about death. His voice was soft, but cold. Strong and sharp like the way wind feels on your face in December. He was an incredibly uncomfortable child to be around and standing near him made you feel like you were cast deep into some shadow—some place completely absent of joy.

"Umm…yeah," I replied. "Why don't you come with me?"

"He's a bad, bad man," the boy said, looking me directly in the eyes. "He is a bad man and he doesn't deserve someone as nice as you. No. Certainly not someone like you."

I felt as though I could have swallowed my tongue. I shook my head, attempting to wake up from whatever dream this was, but no relief came. The boy still stood. He still stared. He still waited for my reply.

"I don't think I know what you're talking about, little man," I said, trying to sound more confident than I was. I went to put my hand on his shoulder to help guide him forward, but he stepped to the side, turned, and faced me once again.

"You know what he did," the little boy said. "You and everyone else around here knows what happened to all those little girls."

"You're talking about Mr. Samuels, I assume."

"Jeremiah is a horrible human being and he needs to be stopped," the boy answered.

"He has been stopped. He can't hurt anyone else any more. I promise. Now if you don't mind, I really do need you to go back downstairs so we can find your…"

"He hasn't been stopped. He hasn't gotten what he deserved and you know that. Why haven't you done anything about it?"

I paused and tried to figure this kid out. I scanned him up and down to see if he had a bracelet on or maybe even a monitoring device. It was apparent that this kid was sick and in need of some serious mental health aid. My impulses wanted to call security or maybe even another nurse, but the thought of him being carried off made my heart hurt. He was a strange little boy, and he frightened the hell out of me, but he was a little boy nonetheless. I didn't want to see him dragged off, even if he was fucking whack-job.

"Mr. Samuels is never going to wake back up. At least not that we know of. And if he ever does, he will never see the light of day again. I don't know why we are having this conversation, but you need to get downstairs right now or else I am going to have to call security. Do you understand me?"

A door opened behind me and I twisted my head around to see who it was. One of the older nurses, a heavy woman in her fifties came through the double doors, carrying a clipboard, reading while walking. Her hair, held stiff with spray, sat on her head like a helmet as she waddled into the hall. I saw my chance and called for her. She looked up from the clipboard, not amused.

"Can you please help me get this young man down to the lobby so he can find his parents?"

She did not respond, but rather shook her head at me and went back to her clipboard. She made her way around me and, to my surprise, the boy was gone.

"Go get some sleep, dear," the blimpish woman said. "I think these hours may be getting to you. But before you do, peek in to check on your patient. Samuels, right?"

She leaned in close to me and began to whisper.

"Between you and me, I don't understand why they won't just let that asshole die, you know? If anyone deserves it, it's him."

A week had gone by and Mr. Samuels still kept on ticking. We had four other individuals pass away that week, which was a rather high amount, even for this ward. But not Mr. Samuels. I'll give it to the sick fuck–he simply would not go into that great light. At this rate, I felt like I would be giving up the ghost before he did. He was going to outlive all of us in this stinking place and I'd bet he was saving up any energy he had left in that wrinkled, decrepit body just so he smile knowing that he stuck it out longer.

I thought about that little boy over and over again. I asked the other nurses who were on duty that evening and none of them said that they had seen a little boy–or anyone for that matter in the ward, especially after hours. I asked the staff from the earlier shift and they told me pretty much the same. There was no boy present that evening and I was slowly going insane. I tried to let my days float by without thinking about him, but there was no victory in it. I needed answers. I wish I hadn't sought them out.

About two weeks after the first incident, Mr. Samuels still breathed and I was still doing these late nights. I carried the calories to Mr. Samuels and sat, looking at him, wondering why he did all of the terrible things he had done. I wondered how a man could have been so sick. I wondered if someone had hurt him. I tried to feel a sense of pity for this dying creature on the bed, but I struggled to think of anything besides the fact that he, more than anyone else in this hospital, deserved to die.

I reached up and touched the man's hand, creeped out by the idea of him waking up or moving, which I knew was impossible.

"Don't do that," said a voice behind me, causing me to scream out loud and drop the clipboard that sat on my lap. I turned around quickly to find the boy, standing in the room with me, watching me reach for the gray man's palm. "If he was still alive, you would be regretting that."

"What the fuck are you doing back in here? Who the fuck are you? How the fuck did you get in here?" I said to the child in an angry whisper, trying to conceal the noise as not to draw attention. "And what do you mean 'if he was still alive'? He is alive! Trust me, I know. It's my job to keep him alive!"

"You need to stop doing your job," the boy said calmly. "Just stop and send him to Hell. For all of us."

"Us?" I asked the child. "Are you one of…one of the kids he…? I thought it was just girls."

"He never touched me," replied the boy. "But if he did, would you feel better about killing him?"

"I'm not killing anyone."

"Just look at it as a favor. To everyone. Think about it."

"I'm calling security."

I reached up and hit the red emergency button that hung over Mr. Samuels' bed. It wasn't the button for security, but rather that connected to the nurses desk–and when a man in a coma hits the nurses call button, it was bound to send people running to the bedside.

The boy took a step towards me. I sunk into my chair, waiting for someone to come crashing through the door. I hit the button again.

Nobody came.

He stepped closer.

I hit the button again.

Nobody.

The boy was standing directly in front of my as he leaned in and whispered in my ear.

"They aren't going to come. Nobody is going to come."

I blacked out.

I woke up drenched in my own sweat; the room was dark

and dusty. I wanted to stand, but felt far to heavy to move my legs enough to rise. I looked around the room, trying to focus on anything within eyesight, but much of the area was blurred by the dust that sifted up through the beams of sunlight coming through the cracks in the blinds.

I hear a rustling sound, like someone moving items around in a junk drawer. The sound of metal clinking filled the air. I see movement from the hallway as a figure shadows the door. It was Mr. Samuels.

He slowly makes his way in and doesn't seem to notice me sitting there. He looks right past me, as he drags his feet towards the wall behind me. He doesn't gaze at me as he passes. Something is shining from his hand.

As he goes around me, I hear a muffled voice, weak and tired. I crane my neck to see what was happening and almost vomited at the sight. Behind me lay a bed, stripped of all hygiene and cleanliness. There were no sheets on the bare mattress, which was filled with holes and dark stains. There, above it, stood Mr. Samuels. Upon it lay a young girl, no older than eight or nine.

He lifted the shiny object from his hand, now quite obviously a blade as it peered through one of the beams of light entering the room. I saw the little girl stir. I closed my eyes and screamed.

———————————

Mr. Samuels didn't make it through the night. It was a

somber moment, but there was no pity. I think people were just happy that it was finally over. The ape was dead, as it were.

As expected, nobody looked much into the death. There was no autopsy. He was just a dead old man with no family or questions left unanswered. I was sitting by his bed when he went. I was sitting there next to a little boy with bright blue eyes as I pinched Mr. Samuels' morphine tube and dumped his calorie meal down the sink.

7

Twenty-Four Hours

The sun burned down the fog that covered the cemetery with a pink hue that morning. The light sat like a puddle, cradled in place by the trees that surrounded the open field of plots which rolled on into the distance, far beyond what Christy could see. The water that collected in her eyes hadn't yet been wiped away by her sleeve as she sat on the cold grass, or rather what was left of it, spaced scarcely across the dark dirt left from boot stomps and elongated standing from the crowds that had come to see the little girl that lay under Christy's feet.

Her name was Robin, or at least that is what the stone slab read.

> ROBIN G. FIRTH
> 2009 – 2015
> BELOVED DAUGHTER,
> GRANDDAUGHTER, AND FRIEND
> GOD BLESS YOU, SWEET ANGEL

There was a picture behind curved glass, already scuffed from the oils of the thumbs of folks who eyes were just as teary as Christy's. Robin was very well-loved and will be very well-remembered. Christy knew this and it brought her comfort.

Christy moved her purse from her shoulder to the ground,

staying silent to maintain reverence, even though she knew that there would be no other visitors–not this early. Not on a Tuesday. Unlike her, most folks had normal jobs. Most folks didn't rely on the tips of well-fed patrons of a run down, Eastern Shore twenty-four-hour diner to supply their rent, utilities, car payments, cell phone, gas, food, and what little else they could possibly need. Not want, but need. Want wasn't an option. This job, the one worked until the wee hours, left Christy with the perfect opportunity to visit Robin alone, well before the crowds that would come in the evening, the sound of youthful death still ringing in their ears.

Reaching down into her burgundy handbag, Christy felt for the smooth wooden handle. Wrapping her fingers around it brought upon the reality of the situation. It was heavy in her hand. The dull steel didn't shine in the morning light. She took a moment to inspect the weapon–to really look over its finer details. What a great piece of machinery it was. No engine. No fuel. Just a combination of working parts that were set off by the manual pulling of a trigger. There was a sort of romance in that to Christy. There was truly something beautiful about the revolver that lay over her palm.

She slid her forefinger over the trigger, just like she had seen in all the movies. This was the only reference she had to the machine's use. She had never fired a gun. She had never loaded one. Thank God for common sense, or she would have never got the bullets in. Common sense and the Internet. Maybe that would be what was written on her stone, if someone had one made.

CHRISTY GOODWRIGHT

1985 – 2015
THANK GOD FOR COMMON SENSE AND
THE FUCKING INTERNET

Christy squeezed her bottom three fingers, feeling just how hard the wooden grip was. For such a cheap weapon–one cheap enough that even she could afford it, mind you–the details of this weapon were rather impressive. The engravings followed the grain of the wood and were certainly not hand carved. One could only imagine the equipment pumping these things out by the dozens...the handles that is, not the guns. Guns are surprisingly hard to get in Maryland, which Christy found out when being turned away from purchasing one from a pawn shop. Even the sleaziest of traders followed the law when it came to guns. Period. The handle warmed up in her fist and she started to grow more comfortable with her decision.

She felt her bicep tighten along with her chest as she slid the gun between her teeth. The barrel wasn't very long, maybe only an inch or so, and she felt that holding the weapon steady with the dull enamel would make for a more successful attempt. It felt like biting down on a spoon, very unnatural and not what she was expecting. She took two deep breaths, knowing that she would pull the trigger on the third.

One.

Two.

The trigger made a clicking noise as the stone feeling went from Christy's throat down to her stomach. She opened her eyes, expecting Heaven, maybe Hell, but either way disappointed to see the hills of the graveyard still before her, her feet now deeper into the soil from the pressure she was emitting. She failed. The gun failed. The ammo failed. Something failed. Something went wrong. Again. Breathe.

One.

Two.

And nothing again. Just the small disappointing *click*. She looked down the barrel and into the chambers of the revolver to be sure that she had loaded all six bullets into the weapon. She had. She counted them out loud, just to be sure. One more time her ivory met the steel. She counted in her head once more.

One.

Two.

She felt a pain in her teeth as the metal jolted away from her mouth. She dropped to one knee, smacking her hand over her lips and touching her teeth to see if any were broken. The gun lay on the ground, directly in front of the dirt pile before the stone. Christy looked up to find a man, dressed well enough to be at church, rubbing his large muscular hand.

"What the devil is wrong with you, young lady?" he asked Christy, dragging his thumb across his palm to sooth it. "Are you simple or something?"

Christy, realizing there was no damage done to her teeth, stared at him wildly. She didn't know what to expect. She didn't know if she understood. Had she died? Was this what the world is like when your gone? Was this man God? Christy came to her feet and took a small step away from the man, brushing off his fine blue jacket before pulling the sleeve of his shirt so that it was sneaking out just a little from under the cuff of the smooth navy.

"Who are you?" Christy asked, now visibly shaking in the presence of this man.

"How's your mouth?" he replied.

"I'm sorry, what?"

"Your mouth. Did you break any teeth? Open up. Let me see."

Without knowing why, Christy opened her lips and bared her teeth for the man to see. He reached forward, forcibly grabbing her jaw, moving her head from side to side then up and down. He used his thumb to pull down her bottom lip, exposing her gums, which were speckled with blood. He pulled his finger across the inside of her mouth and let go of her. He pulled a cloth from his breast pocket and used it to wipe the crimson from his thumb.

"That could've gone a whole lot worse, so you know. Your mouth hurt?"

Christy nodded, her cheeks tightening into an embarrassed scowl, like a little girl being yelled at for making a mess.

"Just think how much it would've hurt if the gun had actually gone off."

Christy's head lifted and she expressed her confusion.

"You mean it didn't?"

"Young lady, are you stupid or something? Don't answer that. I can assume from you actually putting a loaded weapon in your mouth that you must be some kind of stupid. Of course it didn't. You'd be dead. Or worse. You'd be alive but in a whole world of hurt. Like you couldn't even imagine."

"Who the fuck are you?! I'm not stupid! You don't know

anything about me! You don't know what I do or what I've done or..."

"Or what could ever be worth putting a bullet in the back of your throat? You're right. I like breathing without a tube. I like speaking. I like thinking for myself and being able to walk and pick things up and be somewhat productive in my life. So no, I don't know what would be worth discharging a firearm in my mouth. In my world, nothing is worth that. And it should be the same for you."

"Don't you judge me!" Christy yelled, followed by an immediate slumping of her shoulders as she took another step away. "You can't judge me."

"And why not?" the man asked her.

"Because. You're not God."

The man smiled and folded his hands in front of him. He looked up to the sky and let out a deep few bursts of laughter. This sent chills down Christy's spine.

"I'm not God?" he asked.

"No. You're not. I know God and..."

"You? You know God? Well, good gracious, please forgive me, I beg. You know the Almighty! The Alpha! The Omega! You know the Holiest of Hosts and the King of Heaven and Earth! You know Him so damn well yet you still chose to trade this life for damnation? Don't feed me that bullshit. I don't want to hear it. I can judge you all I want. You don't know God. I could very well be God to you."

"So are you God?"

"Don't be stupid again, young lady. Use your brain."

Christy stood silent, still waiting for her answer. The man sighed and put his hands into his pockets.

"I'm not God," he told her. "And you're not dead. Just confused. Very confused. And lucky that I was here to keep you from…that." The man scoffed slightly at the gun on the ground.

"Well, I would say thank you, but I think you can understand that I would really like to be alone right now. I just need some time to…"

"I'm not going to give you that time. Let's make that clear right now."

"Excuse me?"

The man smiled again.

"I'm not going to give you the time. I simply won't. I'm not going to leave."

"You have to leave. I want you to leave me alone."

"No. No I don't."

"I'll call the police!"

"And tell them what? That a man is forcibly keeping you from committing suicide and that they should arrest me on the grounds that I wouldn't let you send your tongue flying out of the back of your head? I don't think they'll bite, if you ask my opinion."

"Fucking leave! I'm serious!"

"Or what?"

Christy bent over and, with a trembling hand pointed the gun at the man, who never flinched or even merely reacted in any way she would have liked him to. He was a stone, stoically staring at her, lacking fear.

"I swear to God I'll kill you right where you stand!" Christy hollered at him.

"Oh, you will?" said the man, taking a step towards the

extended firearm. "You went from suicide to murder just like that? Well then, you best hurry up. Get it out of the way now. Best hope the rest of those bullets work, seeing as how the first two were just so successful."

Christy put the gun to her own head, her hair tangling around the short barrel's iron sight. Her eyes filled with water as she bared her teeth once again, this time not voluntarily.

"Go!" she yelled. "Go or I'll do it!"

"But even if I leave, you'll still do it. What do I have to gain...or lose, for that matter? What is there for me?"

"What do you want from me!" Christy cried. "Why are you doing this?"

"I only want what is best for you. Put down the gun and let's have a little talk, shall we? That sounds nice. An easy little chat. Come on now, hand it over."

Christy removed the gun from her head, pulling out a few strands of her brown hair with it. The man pinched the hairs as he retrieved the weapon from her shaking hand.

"Who are you?" Christy asked. "No more games. Answer the question."

"My name is Walter. And yours?"

"Christy."

"Nice to meet you, Christy."

"Why did you stop me? Why are you here?"

Walter put the revolver on the grave where it was dropped before. He nudged it away with his shiny black shoe, which he promptly brushed off with the back of his hand, bending over at the waist.

"I don't want to see anyone else go. I've seen a bit too much in my time."

"Same here. Which I why I really need to do what I need to do and I really need for you to please leave me to it. It is my cross to bear, dammit. Let me have this. Let me make peace."

"Can I tell you a story?"

"I'm not a child."

"I never said you were. Now may I please tell you a story?"

"Only if you leave afterwards."

Walter stared at her, expressionless for a moment, contemplating her counter offer.

"Fine. I can make that deal," he said. "Do you want to sit?"

"No."

"Fair enough. Then I shall begin. You see, I didn't always have a whole lot–that is to assume that I have a whole lot now, which I very well may not."

"You dress like you have a lot," Christy interrupted.

"The suit can make the man," Walter replied. "No matter what anyone tells you. You have no idea whether I live in a mansion or a cardboard box. You know that I have one good suit at my disposal and that is all."

"You take care of it really well for someone who might live in a box."

"I take care of everything I have," Walter said. "Now please, if I may."

"Sorry," Christy said, looking to the ground again. "Go ahead."

"Thank you. As I was saying, my life wasn't always as grand as it appears. In fact, I'm even willing to tell you that it was quite the opposite. You see, my family did not come from much. We didn't have money or a big house or even enough clothing to put on all of the kid's' backs before we went to school. My mom made us share our clothing and our toys and everything else that a child should have. All four of us, all four boys, only a year or two apart from each other, all with different daddies, none of them ever around. We had to share one mom, one bathroom, one bedroom, one hope or dream to get out of that mess and please believe that one hope split four ways is a pretty dismal thing. We didn't have a single thing that belonged to just one of us. My oldest brother was named Jeremy. He was a bright young man; very good at math. Numbers were kind of his thing, you see. I am sure he would have done so well if he had ended up in college. But he didn't. My brother got himself a little girlfriend and with that came the wanting to impress or do things nice with her or for her or whatever you want to call it. Now, a kid in our situation–even a bright kid like Jeremy–didn't have much to impress this girl-friend with. So Jeremy needed money. And how do young folk from our part of town get money? Drugs. Lots of them. Needless to say he made that money and he did all that could for that girl and please believe that she still left him after a few months just like every other girl at that age does. But now he had the money. And now he had the drugs. And now he also had a nice big red target sitting on his back whenever he would go out with all of his boys. And he had lots of boys. Hard boys. Tough boys. Stupid boys who didn't even begin to understand the things that my brother was capable of. And where there are stupid boys there are stupid decisions and my brother started making them just as quick as he was making that money. He started shooting up that dope-shit and before anyone could even tell him not to, he was strung out all the damn time. He never had a shot to get off of it. My mom put up with it for a little while–she was in denial I think–but it wasn't long before even she got fed up with him. I remember this one time, my brother started to OD in our bedroom and I went and got my momma–I was maybe only eight or nine at the time–and remember her hearing me and just sitting there, looking straight into the wall. It was like she was contemplating whether or not it was worth saving the life of her own son. I'll never forget her face. I pulled her arm and yanked at her wrist to try to get her to follow me down the stairs, but she absolutely wouldn't budge. Not an inch. Her mind was made up at that point I think, and it wasn't in my brothers favor. I had to run outside and find one of my other brothers who was able to call the police, who got the ambulance there, who saved Jeremy's life. Barely. He couldn't move or speak or anything for quite some time. He was restricted to his chair, where he sat day in and day out, seeing as how his brain was so terribly fucked from the trauma. And my mother sat there with him. Not looking at him or talking to him or anything–just sitting there with him, solemnly waiting for an explanation or something. Over time my brother got better. Not fully, but he was able to do some things that he certainly couldn't right after the overdose. He could walk again, which was nice. Not very far and not without his walker, but his legs worked…sort of. He still couldn't use the rest room by himself. Either my brothers or I had to help with that. Same thing with the feeding, which he often spit up. He could lift the fork a few times, but he would eventually get weaker and weaker as the meal went on. It was sad and we knew he hated it. I don't tell you all of this to make you pity him or me or to make you feel bad or something of the sort. I do have a point. You see, my brother was pretty conscious throughout his injury, including his recovery. He knew the stress he put on the family and he knew the burden that he believed he was. He knew his own mother no longer wanted him or cared about him and he knew that his brothers would want to eventually go away to do something with themselves, if they could, seeing as how the hope was only split three ways now instead of four. When I came home one day from school, I noticed that nobody was home. I figured that my mom must have ran to the store which worried me because that would mean that she might have left Jeremy alone in our room. I run into the house to check on him and when I get past the threshold, I see my brother turn his head, a revolver quite like that in his mouth, right before he blew his brains out all over the wall behind him. I didn't get to say goodbye. I didn't get to hear him out nor did he get to hear me. He gargled on the floor, writhing and seizing for about three or four minutes after the gun shot. He didn't try to talk. He didn't try to get up. He just laid on the floor, his finger still behind the trigger-guard, staring at me. I didn't move an inch. I watched him die then sat out front, waiting for my mother to get home."

"That's so terrible," Christy said. "I'm sorry for the loss of your brother."

"It's okay. That was a long, long time ago," Walter replied. "But you can change things around right now."

Christy looked between Walter and the gun, the tears still settling in her eyes.

"I don't think I can," she said. "I don't think I can help it. Please don't get me wrong, I feel awful about your brother and I really wish you all the best–you have my sympathy–but this needs to happen. There isn't any other alternative. I'm sorry, Walter."

"You could just stay with me," Walter said to her, moving his hands behind his back.

"What did you say?" Christy questioned.

"Stay with me. Come with me. Instead of doing this terrible, disgusting thing, why don't you come with me?"

"I don't know! You don't know me!"

"You're Christy. I'm Walter. We do know each other now. So come with me. Leave the gun here. Come on."

"What kind of sick-o are you?" Christy's voice raised as she backed away once again. "Do you stalk the graveyard looking for vulnerable women? That's a sick fucking game and I won't take part in it!"

"Not at all. I'm just trying to give you an option. So come with me. What do you have to lose? You're going to kill yourself anyway, so what does it matter? Just give me twenty-four hours of your time. That's it. Twenty-four hours to prove that I am just a little bit better than hot lead through the skull. I don't think that is asking too much, do you? If you don't think I'm worth it after twenty-four hours, then I will let you come back here or drop you off anywhere in the world you like and let you off yourself with one of my weapons, which I know actually work without fail. It'll get the job done real nice. All of that can be yours if you just give me twenty four hours."

Christy wrapped her hand around the back of her neck. She could feel the blood draining from her face now that she was beginning to calm down. Though the offer was ludicrous, the man had a point. What would she have to lose? She felt her gut twist and the blood rushed back up her body.

"No. I can't. You don't know the things I have done. You don't know who I have hurt and the lives I have ruined. You can be naïve, sir, but I cannot. I simply cannot. Go!"

"Twenty-four hours. That's it. That's all."

"You don't know what I have done. You have no idea."

"Then maybe you need to tell me. I can be the judge of whether or not it is all worth it."

"You're not God."

"And you're no saint, so tell me what happened."

"Okay," Christy wiped her face with her sleeve and attempted to gain composure before taking a deep breath, trying to not continuously look at the gun still lying in the dirt. "It started earlier this year. January twenty-third, to be specific. I have been going through quite a lot. I haven't been able to keep up with work–and that is if I even have a job. Things in life were getting harder and harder. I was married young, but he left me without even telling me why. It was all a blur of black and grey. Everything I did was shadowed by this cloud of depression and so I started drinking. And what was once a week turned to once a day, then to the point of not being able to get through the day without booze. Whiskey, preferably. Jack Daniel's. It's my favorite. So I drank, and I drank, and I made terrible decisions–like the one I made on January twenty-third. I needed to go out to the grocery store, I recall. I don't remember for what at this point, but honestly, that isn't even important. Not in the slightest. I just remember that I need to go out to the store, but with the snow, a lot of places had closed early that day. I knew of one store that was infamous for never closing and, though it was about twenty-five minutes from my house, I decided that I would be the only one on the road, most likely, and that my drinking wouldn't impair me too much. I was hammered, stupid, shit-face drunk. When I came to, I saw the other car on the highway, upside down. I couldn't see the driver–I assume he or she was still in the car, but what I did see was the girl. A little girl, Robin G. Firth, laying out in the red, red snow in front of the car. The windshield was destroyed on the upside down vehicle. The entire scene was a terrifying mess, except my car. I knew I had hit them or at least caused them to go off the road. I could feel the pain in my neck and my shoulders from the seat belt. But I got scared. I got scared and I ran. There was no one there to see it all happen. There was no one there to testify that I was present. There was no one there to save the little girl and the newspapers filled with her obituary the following day. I got away with it. No one ever knew it was me. I have to even the score, Walter. I have to even it all out. Robin deserves that."

"It's not up to you even it all out," Walter said. "It's really not."

Christy stared at the gun and began to bawl, dropping to her knees in front of the revolver. Walter joined her on his knees.

"Twenty-four hours, you said?" Christy asked. "Twenty-four hours or this?"

"That is what I said," Walter replied.

Christy threw herself against his shoulder, crying terribly. As she came up for a breath she noticed the large scar that ran across the back of Walter's head.

"My God." Christy said. "What happened to you?"

She ran her fingers over the cracked webbing of tissue that

molded around Walter's bald skin. The scar took up much of the area behind his skull.

"January twenty-third," Walter said. "Earlier this year."

A gunshot was heard for up to almost half a mile away, but only a few feet from the couple, a tiny giggle could be heard from a young boy with the brightest blue eyes.

8

Rope and Rocks

I was a big fan of rock climbing since I was a little kid. I had always wanted to become a professional, even though it isn't exactly what most would consider a real career. Of course, there are the one-in-a-million guys who get hired by some energy drink company to do something absolutely ridiculous and make a huge chunk of change for it, but for the most part, the guys that do go pro live the life of a raft guide down the New River. It's livable and fun, but doesn't exactly have a 401K for the long haul. Not much lifelong career.

After graduating high school, I went off to college, found a climbing gym, honed in on my skills, trained hard…and finished my degree in business management to land a safe desk job. A cubicle job, rather. I ended up at a boring old insurance company where I would call people and ask them if they would be interested in purchasing life insurance only to get cussed out or screamed at, if they weren't so kind as to just hang up on me before I finished my sentence. The office where I worked wanted to be new and innovative, so they took down all of the walls of the cubes to make an "open-space office" which only made the job more miserable. I do not need to see my desk neighbor picking their teeth for this place to be considered trendy or up to date. But I had no say in the matter so I went in every day and did my job like I was supposed to make my thirty-five thousand dollars per year (before taxes), before heading straight to the climbing gym across town to stay in shape and to dream, just for a few hours at a time.

One of the only positive things that came out of this job was Frank. Frank was a few years older than I and surprisingly was just as into climbing as I am. He did it a lot in college and though he hadn't been incredibly active in the last few years, he still had a membership at a separate gym that he would hit up once a week or so. Once he and I got a bit closer, I was able to talk him into coming over to my gym, it being closer to the office, and actually have a climbing buddy for the first time since school. Frank and I got along great and for the last year dedicated much of our time to the hobby.

Frank had gotten married just before he and I met. His wife was a beautiful young woman who was ceaselessly kind and caring. She had me over for dinner on many occasions and would constantly come to watch Frank and I climb. She was a good woman through and through. Luckily for them, they were successful in their short attempts to have a baby and were eagerly awaiting the birth of their first child when Frank came to me with the idea of an adventure.

"Look man, we have the gear and the know-how." he told me. "The only thing I have a limit to is time. Once this baby is here, there is no way I can get out on the rocks any more. We have never done a full-on climbing trek before. Let's do it before the kid gets here."

His enthusiasm was through the roof and without even thinking about it, I agreed to go. Besides, he certainly wasn't wrong. We both had all of our own climbing gear, most of it professional grade. We both had the experience. We both had the will to get it done. But Frank definitely did not have a load of time, his wife now seven months along. We skipped out on quite a bit of work the rest of the day to sit on our computers and researching prime locations. By quitting time, we knew exactly where we wanted to go.

The weekend of the trip came quick and we drove a few hours out to get to a trail that would lead to the cliffs. The reviews online had said that these cliffs, though slightly dangerous, had beautiful views and were often very available to climbers who didn't want to be bothered with the crowds or hikers that could mess up their climbs. We figured it would be perfect for us. The trail led for about twenty miles into the wilderness. We had taken the day off work on Friday so we could hike out to the rocks, camp for the evening, climb on Saturday, then spend much of Sunday descending before heading back to our normal lives.

We made our way to the cliffs with relative ease. Luckily the trail was rather flat and the terrain pretty easy–or at least easy enough for the two of us to carry our gear packs for the distance without hurting ourselves. Frank and I spent that evening looking over all of our harnesses and carabiners, double-checking the ropes for frays, and all-around making positively sure that everything would go smoothly and as planned. We set up camp and both had troubles sleeping due to how excited we were for the sun to come up. I tossed all night, knowing that I needed to sleep to be one-hundred-percent for the next day, but it felt like I was a kid on Christmas. Unconsciousness finally came to me around two o'clock in the morning.

We packed up and headed towards the cliffs eagerly. I was

physically shaking as we both stood at the base looked up, smiling.

"You sure we're ready for this?" I asked Frank, knowing what his answer was going to be before the breath ever even left his lungs.

"Definitely," he replied without looking at me, still gazing at the behemoth in front of us. "I'm so ready."

We checked our gear one more time and slowly began our ascent. Rock for rock, spike by spike, we made our way up the mountain's sharp edge. I loved the smell of the chalk and feel of the stones under my gloves. Frank was much faster getting up the rock than I was, his harness clinking well above my head. Every so often he would call down to me, double checking to be sure that I was ok. I would reassure him that I was doing fine, which by that point I was, and that I was right behind him.

The wind was not something I had originally anticipated when the climb began. Maybe others were smart enough to expect it, but in my case I needed to learn the hard way. It burned my cheeks and made it more and more difficult to maneuver. As the air pushed Frank and me around, the height of the mountain became more and more evident. This was not a gym. There were no pads on the floor. If something happened or if our gear slipped up, even just once, there was no way for us to be caught or safe...or even alive. There would be nothing to keep us from landing, headfirst, on the hard ground below and painting the mountainside on the way down. I tried to keep these thoughts from my mind as I pulled my shoulders up to my wrists, keeping my frame as close to the stone as I could. All the while, Frank remained fearless and chatty.

"Let me know if you need to take a break down there, brother!" he yelled to me, softly laughing under his breath. The wind was loud, but I was able to hear the tone of his voice just fine and I knew right away that he had no intention of taking a break and was simply trying to be kind. I declined his offer and straightened my legs out to reach the next boulder with my outstretched hand.

After a few hours, I finally got to see Frank crawl over the platform that we had planned to break on. The muscles in my arms and legs all burned, but I was certainly happy to have made it this far. We were over half way up the almost four hundred feet to the summit and I did not expect to be struggling nearly as much as I had. I could not wait to reach the top, where I had every intention on hiking back down the mountainside, even if Frank didn't want to follow. I was not as up for this trip as I had originally intended. I had grown afraid, worrisome, and all-around uncomfortable with what I was doing. This was not what I wanted this trip to be and, though I truly didn't want to ruin anything for Frank, I simply could do much more after finishing the climb–if I made it that far–and even that was just for him.

Frank could tell by the look on my face that I wasn't having fun anymore and, being the generous guy he that he was, offered to climb back down with me if I wanted. I didn't want to kill his good time and I certainly didn't want him to think of me as chicken, so I made up a kind of excuse about possibly having pulled a leg muscle and that maybe, once we reached the top, that I should hike back down instead of repelling; that it would be easier and less impactful. He, of course, disagreed that the walking would be lower impact than the repelling, but understood my concerns and didn't want to give me a hard time. After insisting that we continue, I prepped my harness to continue the climb and tried as hard as I could to refrain from looking down. I could feel the rope moving as Frank started his lifts above me and I clenched my jaw so tight, now stricken with a fear of heights that evolved so suddenly, that I thought I could have bitten off my own tongue.

I slowly inched my way higher and higher, refusing to look to the depths of the valley below, knowing that it would only turn my fear into paralysis. The rocks became more difficult to hold onto with every pull, some even shaking free from their position as my decision making skills seemed to flow out of me with every drip of salty, terrified sweat. I took a few deep breaths and reminded myself furiously that it was almost over. Then I heard Frank call out from above me, just as we were beginning the final overhang.

"What the hell are you doing up here?" he said to some-body, I assumed, as he reached towards the rocks that sprung over the four hundred foot gap of air between itself and the stone below. "Hey! There's a freakin' kid up here! At the top! You see him? Hey kid! What are you doing?"

Frank kept climbing until he crested the top of the ledge. Before I could return any questions in response to an apparent child at the top of the cliff, I feel a loosening of the rope connecting both Frank and me to the rock. I shot a glance up to see Frank barreling towards me, my brain registering the sight before the sound of his screaming. His rope was still attached to the top of the overhang as I heard popping noises from the rock above me. I felt his weight and the momentum of the fall pull me from the stone cliff and I began to swing, hundreds of feet in the air, now joining him in his screaming, followed shortly by tears. I looked up to see that we are both dangling by only one anchor that Frank had put at the edge of the hang and there, leaning over the edge, was the child with brown hair and blue eyes, looking down at the two of us, smiling. With a giggle, he disappeared behind the rock back to safety.

"Frank!" I yelled. "Frank! What happened? Are you okay, buddy?" I waited for a response but none came. I could see Frank hanging below me, but there was no movement. I shook the rope gently, just enough to force it to move a little more than the winds were already moving us. Frank dangled motionless. I called out his name a few more times, shaking the rope as carefully as I could, trying not to disturb our only lifeline at the top of the cliff. The whole contraption, us and all, shifted quickly as I saw the rope slide from Frank's body, revealing the loops that had been wrapped around his throat. Now hanging only from his waist harness, I could see the purple bruising collaring his neck. The child must have wrapped the rope one or two times, rather tightly, before shoving Frank off the cliff.

The anchor above us made a creaking noise as I tried to compose myself, trying not to look down at the corpse hanging from the same lifeline. The anchor budged and the rope slid an inch before catching the two us once again. We were far too heavy. The anchor was giving way. I mumbled prayers and pulled my knife from my belt. I screamed my apologies, Frank not acknowledging my pleas for forgiveness as I cut the only thing keeping my friend from tumbling like a rag doll to the flat rocks at the bottom. His body landed with a loud crack, like that if you dropped an egg on the kitchen floor.

I hung there, sobbing, wondering how this all had gone so wrong, wishing that I would wake up and it would still be the night before the climb so I could wake Frank up and tell him that there was no way in hell that I was going to attempt any cliffs and that I just want to go back to the gym. I begged God to get me out of this or to make it all some sick twist of my own imagination. But after all that had left my lips and my mind, nothing had changed. The body was splattered out below me and I swung from side to side, ready to join the explosion of entrails and bone that used to be my best friend.

I swung myself closer to the cliff's edge, but it eluded my grasp by at least four or five feet. The harder I swung, the more the anchor moved. I screamed out loud with every thrust of my legs, attempting to grab the wall, but not even coming close to success. It was hopeless. I was not going to be able to reach the rock. I grabbed at the rope and tried to pull myself up, to climb the rope itself, but it was no use. I quickly slid down the rope, the friction tearing a hole in my glove. I tried once again, but after making it up a few feet I slid once more, now tearing skin instead of leather. I cried out as I felt the heat in my hands, but I had to keep trying. I gave it one more shot, but the pain was overbearing. I let go and allowed the harness to catch me.

I yelled for help but knew it was worthless. I let myself hang and scream until my throat ran dry and hoarse. Night began to fall and I passed out, hanging from a string like some toy puppet.

I woke up, having soiled myself and feeling incredibly vulnerable. I looked down and saw that wildlife had already dragged off half of my friend below. My tongue felt like sandpaper and the wind had burned my face and my arms. The wounds on my hands had dried up, but were in the opening phases of infection. The sun was coming up over the trees across the valley as I realized that I was not going to be saved. I looked up to see the empty edge of the cliff, hoping that I would see anybody above–even if it was the boy who killed Frank. Nobody appeared. Without tears and without letting out a sound, I took the knife from my waistband once again, knowing what I had to do. I thought to try to swing towards the rock once more, but I needed to save my energy. I needed what little power I had to make it through the thick rope. I said a silent prayer in my head, communicating with the God I hoped I would meet soon enough.

The last thing I saw was the fraying of the rope as the knife dragged across its surface.

9

Knuckles

I should have known that Thomas was full of shit as soon as he opened his mouth. Every time he would go into these deep trances of storytelling, there was always some kind of high-stake, hokey horse crap that would come out instead of anything worth substance. Don't get me wrong, I liked Thomas just fine–more so than most people, to be honest–but I just knew better than to believe any story that started with something like "That reminds me, there was this one time…"

I don't think Thomas really knew that everyone knew that he was a liar. I feel kind of like a bad friend for not ever saying anything to him about it–you know, letting him know that folks no longer thought anything that came out of his pudgy, flapping gullet was true–but I also didn't think it was really my place. As you can imagine, the boy wasn't exactly swimming in friends, couldn't find a lady to sit on his lap if he lost eighty pounds and had million bucks, and wasn't going to have a very easy time next year in college. He was going off to some New England hoity-toity joint that would be full of people very willing to call his bluff–and those bluffs were all he had.

Thomas and I spent a lot of time together, even though most other people would advise me against it. I never worried much about my reputation, though. I knew that I would make out okay, even if the kids here at Gammond High School thought I was a loser for being seen around "Tubbo Tommy." It was their loss. I was a nice guy. They were the ones missing out.

Unfortunately, in our town there really isn't too much going on. They have annual fairs, and they often have weekends where the neighborhood gets together for a giant cookout or something, depending on how warm it is outside before the sun starts scorching over the Maryland tobacco fields (the ones that Thomas says he steals from so he can dry out the plant to make cigarettes–believe it or not, this one is actually true. I smoke a few packs worth of thieving Tommy-brand cigs a month. All for free. Not a bad deal). But besides that, you need to create your own fun around these parts. Probably a big part of why Thomas lies as much he does. Not too many things interesting ever actually go down, besides some small town gossip and Friday night high school football, which I truthfully wasn't that big a fan of.

It was boring here, like much other country regions of the States. It's just the way of life.

I think my favorite story that Thomas tells, and he always tells it, is the story of the house out in Patterson Woods. Thomas likes to believe that he is some type of hero or courageous figure, and this story is supposed to make you believe that, even though we all know it's bullshit.

The story goes that Thomas had heard from someone (no one that we would know, of course) that there was a house out in Patterson Woods that had been left abandoned for decades. Nobody knows who built it or how it still stays standing, but we do know, for certain, that there is something that watches over the house–something not from this world.

Thomas tells us that there once was a man who worked out in those woods long, long ago, before they became the deep, thick forest that they are today. Before there were so many trees, it was mostly farmland, much like the rest of county on this side of the Bay. The man who worked there did so for a wealthy landowner who happened to live in New York City but would come down every so often to check on his property and to be sure that things were running smoothly down south.

Now this wealthy landowner had, as most wealthy landowners did, a very lovely young daughter, maybe only fifteen or sixteen years old. Whenever he would come down to check on his land and the man who worked on it, he would bring her down with him as she seemed to enjoy the ride. One night, while at his estate down here, which obviously doesn't exist anymore and which I am far too lazy to actually look into, he notices that his daughter was not in her room. He goes hunting for her through the dark when he finally ends up at this cabin out in the woods on his property.

In that cabin resides the sole employee of the wealthy landowner on this property.

When he looks into the window, lo and behold, he finds his daughter, naked as the day she was born, sitting on the bedside of that single employee, giggling to herself. It didn't take him very long to realize that she did not like coming to Maryland for the scenic view or the ride out of the city but rather to see this man who, the landowner believed that he could trust.

He went back home and waited for his daughter to come

back. When she did, he locked her in his room and set the manor into flames. There was no neighbor to get to the house in time to save the poor girl and, even though she screamed from behind the locked, heavy door, the landowner refused to change his mind about what needed to be done. He stood there, watching, his brow low over his eyes.

The next day the employee came to the house, hearing of the fire from the night before. He asked the landowner if he was all right and if he knew what had ever become of his daughter and her safety? Than landowner told him that he was unsure if she was able to escape or if she was still alive. He said that he would know as soon as they had cleared the debris.

That evening, the employee had a dream and in it was the young girl, burning alive inside the house, calling for him to save her, condemning her father for what he had done. The next morning the employee went to the landowner and told him of the dream, claiming that he must have known about their affair and killed his daughter in some sick revenge. Obviously the landowner denied the claim but knew that he had been figured out, all because of some dream this man had seen the night after his daughter's death.

To secure the man's silence, while the employee slept, the landowner opened the cabin door and with crude instruments gathered from the kitchen of the cabin, cut out the tongue of the employee then sewed his mouth shut as a warning to never say a word. The employee attempted to break the string holding his lips together, tearing at the flesh and forcing out deep vocal noises.

This angered the landowner even more, yet it also worried

him. He went back to the remains of the manor, leaving the employee on the cabin floor, writhing in pain, only to return with his hounds. It took only seconds for the dogs to tear the man limb for limb, leaving nothing but his blood as evidence.

The story goes that two horrendous ghosts will meet anyone who attempts to stay the night in that house. The first is that of the daughter who appears only for a short period of time, mostly in quick flashes like the flames that consumed her. The second is of the employee who seeks out his vengeance on the landowner, his mouth sewn shut, torturing the men or women who attempt stay in his house before viciously slaughtering them, never to be seen again.

Thomas is, as far as we know, the only survivor of such an evening. That's right: our very own Thomas is the only man to ever escape with his life.

Why Thomas ever thought that anyone in their right mind would believe that shit is beyond me, but I will admit that he did a great job of telling the legend, even if no such house ever existed. It surprised me that he could make something up so creative, especially since he is guy who still has to cheat on his critical responses in even his low-level English classes, which he hates admitting that he is still in, even as a senior. My guess is that Thomas heard the story from some television program or maybe even another student here in town and reworked it to make it his own. But in his version of the story, he made himself the surviving hero.

He describes to us all the awful noises made by the girl who appears very quickly. He says that she makes you jump every time she appears and her skin is leathery and wrinkled, blackened by the heat. She is the only warning you are granted before the ghost of the employee comes knocking.

Thomas says that the key to surviving is staying inside the house until the sun comes up. The employee's ghost won't come into the home where he was mutilated and killed. He stays outside and torments you until you leave to get away, only to catch you and send you down into a violent oblivion. Once you're outside, there is no way to escape. You need to stay in the house, block the doors and windows, and pray that he doesn't drive you mad.

After hearing this story enough, I finally decided to see if there was any merit in what he was saying, even though I knew for a damn fact that there wasn't. I asked him where in the woods the house was and if he would be willing to stay in it again with me. He said that there was no way he was ever going anywhere near that house, even if it was just to show me where it was. He also told me not to bother looking for it because it is too terrifying and that he cared about me. He didn't want me to be next.

When I asked if he could just tell me where in the woods he found the house, he simply couldn't remember (of course) but made up something about following a small stream, he thinks, until the path trails off into nothingness. If I was to keep going, I would find the house.

Now, there must be a hundred or so streams in this damn forest and even more trails, so I knew that he was just covering tracks, but since it was a nice evening, I decided to play along and told him that I would be going to the house if he wanted to join me. I could see the concern in his eyes as he asked me not to, even though the concern was more selfish than genuine. This was a young man who didn't care about my safety but instead cared about being caught in a lie. Little did he know that I wouldn't snitch him out if the place were a fraud. I knew that it was before stepping foot into the woods. I just thought it would be a good way to spend the night.

With Thomas double-checking to be sure this is what I wanted to do, he told me to call him if I needed anything and to keep him posted. I didn't tell him that I wouldn't have my phone on me, seeing as how I knew the service out in this part of the county was absolutely terrible. They simply don't put towers out in towns of only a few hundred folks—none worth keeping up with, I suppose.

I waved goodbye to Thomas and started into the depths of the forest, just as the sun was getting ready to go down. Now I will say, I was certainly surprised at how frightening these woods could be at night. As I walked, I start to let the story dig deeper into my brain and I began to regret my midnight wandering, even if it was even scarier for Thomas, awaiting my return and the calling of his lies.

It was easy for me to create a path that was similar to the one described by Thomas. I followed one of the many streams that ran parallel to a path until the stream turned into a pond of muddy water, seeming to sink into the ground. I continued down the trail until it ended, using the flashlight I brought with me to inspect every noise I heard in the woods, hoping not to run into a bear or a wolf, both of which were lurking in these parts. It wasn't too uncommon for farmers to have to spook the wolves away from their sheep, and these woods would be the perfect hiding place for them.

I kept pushing forward into the dark until a small flicker

caught my eye about fifty yards ahead. I couldn't believe it when I saw it.

Sitting in the middle of the trees was a small cabin, maybe only two or three rooms, with a candle in the window.

A snapping sound came from behind me, mustering up enough of a reason for me to move towards the house and maybe even knock on the door. As I approached, I realized that I could see clear into the windows. The candle did well at lighting up the small space and, without any real effort, I could tell that the cabin was empty. I peered in through each window, the rooms only bearing a few pieces of old, dust-covered furniture and no person in site. I scanned the area, looking for whomever lit the candle but with no success. I grabbed the doorknob and twisted, the door coming open in my hand.

The air in the cabin made me step back, filling my nostrils with a thick coating of musky particles. I shook my head, clearing my airway, before slowly creeping into the house, shutting the door behind me.

"Hello?" I whispered, curious to see if someone would speak back. "Is anybody in here?"

I was certain that the place was vacant, but I couldn't quite get how the candle was lit if this house was abandoned. Everything in the cabin was covered in dust, completely untouched. Then it hit me.

Thomas.

That son of a bitch was setting me up the whole time. I couldn't believe that I had let him get the best of me. All the crock about being concerned for me and telling me not to go–he was priming me to explore the whole damn time. Clever, you bastard.

"Come on out, Thomas!" I hollered. "I know it's you."

I waited for a response but none came. I stood by the doorway, anxiously anticipating movement or a "Boo!" from my tubby buddy, but the silence stayed unbroken. Once again, I called out to him.

"Thomas, I know you're up to this. The story and the description–man, you outdid yourself! Come on out now and let's go home. I could use a cigarette and I bet you could, too!"

Silence still.

I decided to take a seat on a long, brown chest that lay next to the door. There was no response from anything. Not even a cricket chirp. I could see the light dancing along the wall from the candle in the other room. It seemed somewhat brighter now. Not incredibly bright, but far too much for a single candle. As I watched, the light got even brighter. Thomas was in the other room and I was going to get the upper hand on him now.

I quietly made my way along the wall, crouching as though I was in an action movie. All the while, the light grew brighter and brighter, no longer dancing on the wall, but instead taking it over, filling the room with a bright orange and yellow hue. I jumped into the doorway, ready to yell his name to make him jump, but was knocked onto my back by what I saw.

For a brief moment, maybe only a second or two, there stood the figure of a young woman, her skin scarred and bubbling as her mouth hung open as if she were trying to scream. I could see the pain she was in and feel the heat from the fire that surrounded her. And within a second she was gone.

"What the hell!" I said loudly, picking myself up off the ground. "No fucking way!"

There is no way that Thomas could have been telling the truth. I walked in towards the room, wondering how the hell that could've happened. The candle was still lit, so I picked it up and looked for some kind of projector. The brass candlestick was cold in my hands as I flung it around the room. Nothing. Nothing at all. Whatever trick Thomas was pulling, he was doing one hell of a job. Good for him.

I decide that it is time for me to leave, wanting not to be scared any more than I already had been. I'll let Tommy have this one. He wins. I just want to go home. I lean in to put the candle back on the sill, looking at my reflection in the glass of the window, adjusting my hair which had become disheveled in my jump scare. I blew out the candle only to feel the air get stuck in my throat.

Leaning into the glass, looking directly at me was the tattered face of a man, his eyes no longer in their sockets, blood dried across his cheeks, hair torn from his head. The most distinguishing feature, however, was that his mouth was crudely sewn shut with thick, yellow, pus-covered cord. I could see him trying to open his mouth, but the cord was too strong to give way. I scurried back away from the window, kicking for dear life. I started to scream. Then the man began tapping.

Tap-tap. Tap.

He began rapping his knuckle on the window. I could feel tears swelling under my eyelids before escaping down my face. He stared straight at me with the empty sockets.

Tap-tap-tap.

He left his knuckle pressed against the window, still staring. I slowly tried to back away through the door.

Tap. Stare, pushing the glass. *Tap.*

I stood to my feet, looking out the other window, wondering how much longer until the sun came up. Couldn't be too much longer, I thought to myself. I had been out here for quite some time and it was summer so the sun would be up early. The window behind me starts making noises. I turn to find him tapping yet again.

Tap-tap. Tap.

Tap-tap-tap. The rattle of the glass as he pushed against it so hard matched my shivers.

Tap. Stare. *Tap.*

I moved back into the other room, looking for things to throw over the windows. I had to stay until the sun came up. I couldn't run. I knew that he would stay and torment me until then, but if I tried to leave, he would destroy me. He followed me back into the first room, staring in from the windows, tapping on the glass, messing with my brain. This continued for what felt like hours, until I saw, just beyond the trees, a glimmer of light from the sun. He would follow and tap and, when I would rest, he would stay at the window, looking at me and tapping–tilting his head like a questioning dog.

I walked up to the window, just as the rays of light began to illuminate his skin. I smiled at him, knowing I had won. It was only then that I noticed the expression on his face wasn't that of anger or pleasure, but rather similar to the one that Thomas had just as I had left into the woods. Genuine concern. Once again he rapped on the window, as his body began to tremble.

Tap-tap. Tap.

Wait a minute. Had all of this been the same pattern? His knocks were slow and intentional now.

Tap-tap-tap. The pressure from his knuckle holding down that last tap was surely going to break the window.

Tap. Stare. *Tap.*

I placed my hand against the window as his body began to lower. I could see that it was getting hard for him to stand. He repeated his rhythm and I thought about the hours I had spent studying Morse Code in Boy Scouts many years ago and began to tremble even harder than he.

Tap-tap. Tap.

R.

Tap-tap-hold.

U.

Tap. Hold. *Tap.*

N.

He began to shake his head softly, defeated, and turned away, hiding his face from the window as not to see whatever was going on in the window. I didn't want to turn around, even when I could hear the snarky laughter of a man, growling of dogs, and what I believed to be the chuckle of a young boy in the house.

This thing wanted to send me a warning. He wanted to save me. I didn't listen.

They had been in the house all along.

10

Remember

Where am I? I thought, trying to sit up. A forceful push knocked me back down onto a mattress. I put my hands out in front of me, reaching and gripping at nothing. It was dark. Pitch black.

"Where am I?" I hollered out loud this time. "Why is it so dark in here? Answer me! I can hear you!" I started swinging my arms to defend myself against the invisible monsters in front of me.

"Sir, I need you to calm down. Listen to me. It's okay. You're okay. My name is Dr. Callaway. You were in an accident. Luckily someone found you in time. They were able to pull you from the car and revive you. We weren't sure if you were going to make it. But it's okay now. I just need you to take a few breaths and calm down. You took quite a hit on the head. What do you remember?"

I tried to think about any recollection of an accident, but came up with nothing. I tried to remember anything before the accident and, horrifyingly, couldn't remember a single thing.

"What's my name?" I asked, now trembling. "Who am I? What's going on? Holy shit."

"Things like this aren't uncommon, sir," the doctor said. "You got quite the bump. Just relax."

"How can I relax? I can't see. I can't remember anything!" I yelled, now starting to cry. As I started paying attention to the sounds around me, I could tell that I was in a hospital room. The beeping of a heart monitor was repeating itself close by. I heard the shuffling of feet and the clinking of metal instruments. I gripped the rails at my side, confirming that I was, in fact, in a hospital bed.

I tried to calm down and remind myself that I was going to be okay. That's what the doctor said. I think that's what the doctor said. I couldn't really recall his exact words. I'm alive, which is good.

"Now, you aren't reacting to any light tests here," Dr. Callaway said. "Can you see anything in your eyes right now?"

"No. No, I can't. What's going on?" I replied.

"I can assume you had your eyesight before this, correct? You were in the driver's seat of the car involved in the accident."

"Yes. I think. I believe so," I said.

"Okay. That's fine. These things sometimes happen. You should hopefully be getting your vision back in time. Just make sure you let us know if you think you begin to see anything, okay? We have quite a few scans and tests to run, which may give us more answers. I tell you what, young man–you're incredibly lucky. I know it might not seem like it right now, but you truly are."

I laid my head back onto the pillow, attempting to allow myself to trust the man who voice kept talking to me. I shut my eyes, then opened them, expecting change. How foolish. Still dark. Again. No difference. I sighed and left my eyes shut, trying to tune out the sound of the doctors talking in medical jargon amongst themselves.

I am finally getting used to my cane. I think. It's hard to gauge. I can only assume I am getting better with it because the bruises on my shins are finally starting to not hurt anymore due to the fact that I am not regularly slamming into the ends of low tables and chairs. I haven't tripped down steps in a while and have started to understand the way that the hospital is built–at least spatially. The last two weeks, according to Dr. Callaway, have been impressive.

I don't remember much from the past. I remember certain small things–things which seem unimportant until they are the only things you can remember. I remember that my name is John. I remember that I am thirty-one years old. I remember that I graduated from college, but I don't remember from where. I don't know my friends' names, if I had any, and I don't remember where I lived before this hospital. They were able to tell me more from researching my car registration, but honestly, it doesn't matter much right now. Again, those things are only important if you can remember the story of "John." If not, then it all might as well be fiction. A freakin' storybook. A lie.

Dr. Callaway says that if I keep up with my good results, I might be able to go home soon. I pretended to be decently excited for this, but the house means nothing to me–it'll be just as new in my mind as the day I bought it. I just hope I still like it. More so, I hope I left it clean. The doctor also tells me that I should start to remember more little things as the weeks go by. The big stuff, like the world around me, I get. I know what a car is, I know not to walk into the street (if I can help it using my cane), I know that planes fly, that I am supposed to eat food (except shellfish, since I am allergic, apparently), and all that shit. I just struggle with details, but what I have is enough to qualify me to live on my own.

I go to bed every night in my room, which is the third on the left after stepping off the elevator, but not the one with the curtain drawn. That room belongs to Bruce. He is kind of an asshole and gets mad if my cane crosses his threshold. His voice sounds like a young man until he is mad, mainly at me or the doctors, which is when you can tell his age. He's shrill when he talks. I don't care much for him. He had a head wound, too. He fell off a horse or something. I often hope that he wasn't like this before his accident. I can't imagine that he was because people still come and visit him, which I imagine wouldn't be the case if he wasn't a nice person before his incident.

Regardless, he is an asshole now.

I closed my eyes, now used to the lack of change between sleeping and waking, and tried to dream again which, though seldom, happened still in color.

Green was my favorite to see. But there wasn't any green tonight.

I dreamt I was standing in a desert. I could feel the heat of the sun. It was noon or close to it. There was nothing but brown and orange dirt for miles with the exception of this faded grey concrete road that stretches on forever, just like you see in the movies. It was silent in the dream except for the sound of the wind grazing over my ears. I am staring down the road at nothing until I hear some heavy breathing behind me.

I turn to find a car–I can only assume it is mine–an older model Volvo station wagon. It was covered in that same copper dust as the earth around me. And behind it was a woman, slowly moving away from the car, away from me, into the desert, dragging her leg as she took each step. There was bright red blood seeping from her light blue jeans, which were torn and tattered. Her face was one of terror as she tried to run from the car. I could hear her sobbing as she tried to fight her way into the desert.

Then I woke up.

I mentioned the dream to Dr. Callaway who only made a humming noise as I told him. He mentioned that there could be a chance that the dream had something to do with my memory, but it could also just be a cinematic bit of work I had created in my head. He didn't want to think too much of at the moment and essentially told me to chalk it up to simply a 'nightmare.'

It was a nightmare I had over and over again. I remember what a nightmare was from the past and I even remember that I had them terribly when I was very little–nothing in detail, but I remember, I suppose, the idea of nightmares and having them when I was young more than anything. These nightmares, however, were exactly the same, night in and night out. No details ever changed. By this point I could almost draw them out, frame for frame. Always the desert, always the girl, always the car and the orange dust. Always the blood and running.

I told my doctor that they kept happening and he would consistently dismiss it until one day, shortly after I woke up, the doctor anticipated my retelling of the same old story, but this time brought a psychologist with him, hoping she could shed light on my story. I told her everything and, even though I couldn't see it, I knew this woman was shaking her head. I could feel it.

"Why are you upset with me?" I asked her. "Did I say something wrong?"

"Not at all," she replied. "What do you think the dream means, John? Is there any significance to the woman? The car? The road? Any of it?"

"You tell me!" I said, beginning to allow my frustration to shine through. "Isn't that your job? Aren't you supposed to fill me in on what is going on in my brain?"

"No one knows your brain like you do, John," Dr. Callaway spoke up, breaking the tension between the psychologist and me. "That's why all the questions are being asked. If it is too much, we can try again some other time. I was just hoping that maybe having Dr. Jones here to help you analyze might get you started on jogging your memory or pulling something from the dream."

"It doesn't. I'm sorry," I said back, quietly. "And nobody wishes that it did more than I do."

———————

Time passed and I got much better with being blind. I was able to use my cane and, even though I still haven't left the hospital, I knew how to use this bad boy with expert precision. Or so I believed.

I no longer heard from Bruce, the mean, nasty man that stayed in the room next to mine. One day I heard some men enter his room in the middle of the night and when I woke up the morning, he was gone. I asked Dr. Callaway if he had turned out okay and Dr. Callaway assured me that he was getting the upmost care where he was heading and that he was ready to join others again outside of the hospital. Since Bruce was gone, I asked him what happened to him and if he was as bad off as I was. I was told that he stole a police horse and rode it for a few miles before it kicked him off and stepped on his head. I cringed at the thought and promised Dr. Callaway that I wouldn't tell anyone he told me, to which he said that it was okay. Apparently, I would have been able to guess that much for myself if I was able to see him. He might as well have still had the horseshoe attached to his dome.

I asked Dr. Callaway when I would be able to go home again, and he said he wasn't sure. He had told me 'maybe' just a few weeks ago, so I was curious about how the change came about. Dr. Callaway told me that it was nothing to worry about and that I should just try to relax and get my memory back as best I could. I agreed and reminded him that I was trying.

The dream didn't change and was beginning to haunt me more and more. I asked Dr. Callaway to speak with Dr. Jones again, promising to be a little more accepting of her practice and willing to work with her this time. He agreed to get her for me and, within an hour, I was sitting in her office. I could tell it was quite a ways from the normal part of the hospital because it was much warmer in her office than the wing where my room was. I was still wearing my gown that I kept on all the time, so I knew I hadn't gone outside at all. I was eager to feel what my cane was like on concrete. It made me both nervous and excited when I thought about it.

Dr. Jones sat me down and asked if she could get me any-thing. I declined and allowed myself to sink into the plushy couch across from her next to Dr. Callaway. I could hear another person in the room with me and immediately asked who they were. Dr. Jones told me that it was just a friend of hers who was leaving. With this she asked the other person, whom she called Joseph, to let them be for a little to talk. There was a moment of silence before the door opened and this Joseph character exited the room.

"Do you often have friends hanging around your office when you have patients?" I joked with Dr. Jones. I felt that might have been out of line, but hoped that my face showed her that I was only playing around with her. I honestly didn't care that Joseph had been there. I'm sure he was a fine person and I'm sure he wouldn't have cared about my dreams.

"Believe it or not, I do. It's a strange setup, you know?" she said back to me, joking along. I smiled at this response, even though Dr. Callaway cleared his throat, showing that he might not have been amused at our banter. "So tell me, John, has anything changed in your dreams since we last spoke?"

I shook my head no.

"Well, have you noticed any more details?" she asked me. "Sometimes details are the most important part, even in the repetition."

"I know that whatever happened to this woman was bad. She is obviously afraid of something and running from some-thing. I often times wonder if it is me, but I know that I didn't do anything to her. I can't imagine that it's me. Shit, if I could, I'd try to help her. I can't move in the dream. I just kind of exist."

"Does anything in the dream look familiar to you?"

"Yes, actually. Well, kind of," I start. "The car. It's this old Volvo. I want to say that it is my car, but I'm not sure."

There is silence.

"Believe it or not, John, you're correct. That was your car," Dr. Jones said. "Good job. Anything else from the scene stand out to you?"

"Just the car and the woman. There really isn't much around the area. It's just road and dirt. Lots and lots of desert dirt. I think that's the scariest part of the dream. It's obvious that the woman wants to get away from something, but where in the hell did she think she was going to go? There is nothing around her for miles. Even if she took the road, she would be out in the sun–out in the desert for hours and hours before she got anywhere. And with that limp she's tending to, she wasn't going anywhere any time soon. Especially if she was being chased." There was another silence, this time it was longer. "Did I say something wrong?"

"No," Dr. Jones said. "Not at all. Does anything ever happen after you see the woman trying to get away? Does she ever fall or do you ever move around the scene?"

"Never," I reply. "I always wake up."

"Okay," Dr. Callaway said. "Dr. Jones, is there anything else you would like to ask John?"

"No thank you, doctor," she said back, sounding defeated.

"Wait!" I said sharply. "That's all? Like, that's it? We aren't going to talk about anything else a little more?"

"Do you know anything else?" Dr. Callaway said to me in a frustrated tone.

"I suppose not, but wouldn't it help to try?"

"Not today, John," Dr. Callaway said. "Let's get you back to your room."

He handed me my cane, and we headed back to the cold wing of the hospital.

———————————

I started getting antsy in the week following my appointment with Dr. Jones. There was a new patient next to me. He was a young boy who very rarely spoke. I wasn't able to catch his name. Whenever I asked him, he would just giggle and say something snarky. I didn't care much for him, but at least he wasn't as big of a dick as Bruce was. I would always hear the boy leave any time my doctors came around, which I hadn't realized until then, but I really appreciated. It was nice knowing that there wasn't someone who could hear the conversation through the paper thin wall dividers in the hospital.

The dream came and went and I would ask Dr. Callaway for more time with the psychologist, but he refused. I asked if there was a set time for me to leave the hospital, but he told me that I wasn't ready to leave and that there were more tests to take. I would have scans done from time to time, but I never recalled ever getting any more information from them that I had in the past few months. I was never too agitated with my stay in the past, but I fell like that was fueled by that fact that I didn't know any different. Now that I had started to think that I missed the outside world–and having been told I wasn't allowed back out into it–I was slowly getting more and more upset that I spent every day inside this hospital.

I decided that I should just get up and try to leave. I figured if I made the attempt during the day, that Callaway or one of the nurses would see me and try to stop me. I think I knew my way around the building well enough that I could find the front door, even without having been there before. I could always tell it was nighttime by the lack of staff that wander the hallways outside my room, so I figured that, once Callaway went home for the day and once I was left by myself for a bit, I would be able to get up and get on the move, even if just to go outside for a few minutes. What's the worst that could happen?

I waited for the time to come and I could hear the boy next door shuffling back into his bed.

"What you doing over there, young blood?" I asked him, trying to drum up a little conversation.

"They're gonna fry you, ya know," he said. "They're gonna fry you real good."

"What the fuck did you say, kid?" I asked him. "Who the hell do you think you're talking to? I didn't like using such language around a child but that is not something to joke around with.

"As soon as the trial is over, they're going to put you in the ground." he said, still giggling. "They don't let people like you out of here."

"Who do you think you are? I'm not going to let you speak to me that way!" I said to the kid. "Do I need to call a nurse in here?"

"Won't do you any good," he replied. "You're not even a human being to them. They don't care about you. They don't care about what you say. They and the rest of the world know what you've done."

"What's your name, punk? I'm getting the nurse and having you moved."

"You can tell them whatever you like. It doesn't mean anything at all. Not coming out of your mouth, at least."

"What's your name?" I asked, furiously.

"Andrew," he told me, giggling.

His laughter brought out a fire in me and I hollered for the nurse as loud as I could. I hollered two or three times until I finally heard footsteps rush to my room.

"Are you okay, sir? What's wrong?" the young woman asked me.

"Can you please tell the little shit next to me to shut his fucking mouth! He keeps saying these awful things about how they're going to fry me and that I'm going to die and shit like that. I can't tolerate it. Move him or move me, I don't care, but I won't be treated like that!"

"Sir, there isn't anyone in the room next to yours." the nurse said. "It's been empty since they took Mr. Connor off to general."

"What do you mean 'to general'?"

Just then I heard another set of footsteps come towards my room followed by a scuffle and some angry whispers.

"What did you say to him?" an older woman asked, trying to keep me from hearing. "What did you tell him?"

"Nothing!" the young nurse replied. "He asked about a kid next to him and I told him that no one has been in there since they took Bruce Connor back to general population."

"General population?! Someone tell me what the fuck is going on! Now!" I yelled at the top of my lungs, reaching for my cane.

"Calm down, sir," the older nurse said, grabbing my arm. "I need help in Six, please!"

More footsteps–heavy ones–followed her call and I was soon grabbed by large figures with deep grunting tones in their voices. They held me down, just as I heard the older nurse instruct someone to call Dr. Callaway.

When Callaway arrived, he pulled up a chair next to me and instructed the men to let me go.

"What's going on, Doctor?" I asked him. "I want to leave. I want to leave now. You can't hold me here against my will as a patient. I am going home! Now!"

"Relax, John." Callaway said. "Chill out or they will call security back on you, and nobody wants that, okay?"

"Get me out of here. Right now!" I ordered.

"I'm afraid it isn't that easy, John. I'm sorry."

"You can't hold me here! I refuse your service! I know I have forgotten much of…everything…but I KNOW that you can't keep me in a hospital if I refuse the service you offer. I know I am allowed to leave!"

"That would be the case if you were in a normal hospital, John, but you're not." Callaway sighed. "You have been in Central State Hospital for Federal Prisoners since you woke up. Your living quarters have never changed and weren't going to until you remembered what happened, why you're here."

"What are you talking about?" I said to him. "I'm no criminal. I haven't done anything wrong. This is a mistake. You need to get me out of here."

"You are a criminal, John. You just don't remember. We wanted you to remember. We figured it would be so much easier if you did. We tried to avoid this moment–having to say something to you before it all came back. Nobody thought that it would come down to this. Now, here you are, making up kids in empty rooms to..."

"I'm not making up anything! There was a boy in the other room who was saying I was going to fry! Am I going to fry? Is that what is happening?" I started to panic to the point that I struggled to breathe. "Was the boy telling the truth?"

"There is no boy," Callaway said. "This is a prison. There was never any boy. Period. And we aren't sure, but it doesn't look good. You are, in fact, facing the death penalty."

"Why haven't I been to trial? I know my rights!"

"What trial would you like, John?" Callaway said, reaching for my hand. "You don't even remember Sarah. You don't know who she was."

"Sarah?" I replied. "Is that the girl from the dream?"

"We think so," said Callaway. "You found out she was having an affair. You didn't want to face that as a fact and, apparently, you had seen enough of it. You walked in on her with a friend of yours–a Mr. Gary Smith. You killed him with a knife from the kitchen in your bedroom."

The name Gary Smith rang a bell. I couldn't place my finger on it, but the name made me furious. It stirred up a fire in me that I couldn't understand. It was like a breeze in a closed room.

"No," I said to Callaway. "No. I would never kill somebody."

"You then, from what we can tell, asked your wife to get dressed and took her to the car. You drove her out to the desert where you attacked her in the front seat of the vehicle. She tried to escape, but was badly hurt by your knife."

"The dream," I said. "She was running from me."

"That is correct," Callaway told me. "When she started to run, you got back in your car and ran her down. Multiple times. We believe that you would not have stopped if, just beyond her body, there were no ditch. The one you drove into. The one that caused you to smack your head on the wheel. A passer-by found your smoking vehicle and the remains of your wife shortly following. You were in the drivers seat. The knife was on your lap. You were covered in her blood. I'm sorry, John."

I tried my best to remember anything at all at this point. My head throbbed as I pushed the blood to it, shaking.

"They're going to fry me, aren't they, Doctor?" I asked. "I killed her and they're going to kill me right back."

"It looks that way," Dr. Callaway said softly. "Now would you like to go for a walk?"

11

Store

I have been managing this pet shop for what feels like an eternity–and I fucking hate it. Everything about his place makes me sick to my stomach and I often spend nights at home wondering what in the world I did to end up here. If I had known this is where I would end up at thirty-nine years old, I would have paid more attention in school. Maybe picked up a trade. Gotten more into computers. I don't know, something. I certainly wouldn't have let myself get here. If only I had known.

I spend most of my days doing exactly the same thing, over and over again. I wake up, drink my coffee, get into the store, make sure there is some snot-nosed teenager at the counter and that everything is stocked for the day, and then wait for my nine to ten hour shift to be over. Day in and day out, it is just me sitting around, waiting for my shift to end. Nothing exciting really happens. Ever. Once in a while a kid will come into the store and knock something off the shelves and I have to get one of the staff to go sweep up the dog food or maybe set the chew toys up to look more appealing, but that is the craziest kind of thing that ever happens.

You would think that someone like me, who absolutely loves…well, loved, animals would be thrilled with a job like this. Most people seem to think that when you work at a pet store, especially these larger ones, you get to spend your days playing with puppies and kittens or you get to help the animals in our veterinary clinic that is attached to the front of the store, but if people could spend the time in the shop, they would quickly see that this gig is not anything close to what it's cracked up to be. I started here quite some time ago, thinking the exact same thing. I saw the commercials with all the smiling dogs and happy, dance-type music with the bells and fell into he trap of cheerfulness. This place is nothing like the commercial. It's all animal shit and barking and piss and everything else foul in this world under one big roof covered in fluorescent lighting. I had never seen a dead dog until I worked here and now it doesn't even faze me. The vets put down dogs every week. There is never a shortage of fourteen-year-old pups that need that final nap. It used to break my heart, every single time. Now I shrug at it.

I blame this place for a lot of my problems, but my coworkers will say that there are quite a few things in my life that may have led to my outlook on the world. My wife's passing really took a toll on me and, though I tried my best to hide how I felt over the last six months, I can't say that I have always been successful at it. Your world changes quite a lot when someone close to you is gone, especially someone that immediate. The funeral and services all seemed to happen so fast and before I knew it, she was in the ground and I was filling out more paperwork than I ever thought possible. I would have to go back to being just me again instead of us. The thing that I found interesting about it though was the fact that the folks that hand you all of that paper, the folks at the funeral homes–the ones who want your money when your family croaks–they all seem to have the same understanding of human death that I have about dogs: they all die and you just have to be there to see it. There was something oddly justifying about this.

I did have a good feeling about today. I could tell that today wasn't going to be so bad. Today was interview day and I absolutely love interview days. Well, the interviews themselves, at least. The days can still be taxing. I had set up an appointment for eleven in the morning with this woman named Allison and she was going to be convincing me why she would make a wonderful sales associate here at the store. I was originally thrown off by the fact that she was older than our normal hired employee – this woman was, from what I could guess while doing a little social media research, around twenty-five, but admittedly a rather attractive young lady with a bright, gleaming strip of pearly whites across her face. I know if she got the position I sure wouldn't mind having someone like her to look at. Not that I would ever think to make any advancements. I have been to far too many HR trainings that reminded me just how wrong it is to flirt here at work and, not to mention, I'm not even going to try to pretend that even if it was a good idea to flirt around here that I was anything remarkably within this woman's league.

No, you see, I could tell just by looking at her that she was the type who was into the guys with the full head of hair and the deep-cut muscles across their stomach–of which I have neither. I could pick out that she still liked to go to bars and drink and party with her friends on weekends and I could tell that she would be the first to tell a guy to fuck off if he ever had anything negative to say about her, even if he was just trying to get her attention like a lot of the young, stupid boys do nowadays. Allison was beautiful in every conventional way, but I could tell she was made of gasoline, flint, and steel. And this excited me because for those few minutes, whether she got the gig or not, I was going to be in control. This was the only part of the job I actually liked. It's not that I look to play with her strings or fool with anyone's emotions for that matter, but I can tell you right now that there is no feeling in the world that makes you feel more accomplished than having someone actually call you 'sir' for a change, laugh at all your jokes, and frankly, kiss your ass for just a little bit to burn off some of the elongated boredom that flooded every single day in this building. Allison was going to be arriving within a few hours and for the thirty minutes she is in my office, I get to feel as though I am of some importance–like I am the shot-caller for a change, even if the shots being called involve doggy diaper shelf placement.

I stand towards the front entrance, trying not to seem too eager for her arrival. I didn't want her to think that I was waiting for her, even though I certainly was. Not so much for her as much as for the event itself. I paced the length of the storefront, back and forth, counting my steps as I went to pass the time. Forty-two steps it took to get from one side of the shop to the other. As I paused to turn and repeat my tracks in front of the clinic, I was almost toppled over by a small boy standing in front of the veterinarian's office door. I dug my heels into the tile as best I could to keep from falling over him and I immediately began to apologize, asking if he was alright and if I could help him. The boy said nothing at all and simply stared at me with his large blue eyes. I asked him again if he was all right and still he just stared, wide-eyed and stoic, his hands in

the pockets of his battered old overalls. This goofy-dressed little shit was trying to play with me. I was just on the verge of
getting loud when I looked up through the window of the vet
clinic to see that there was a couple, sitting and crying outside
of the enclosed second room beyond the glass. I knew exactly
what that meant and, though my sympathy for the tragedy is
not what it used to be, I did feel bad for the boy who was
more than likely in some type of shock. That would explain
his strange behavior. I looked back to him, then back through
the window, then finally back at him again before nodding my
head and moving on with my steps and my counting. Forty-
two. Every time. I heard the bell go off as another customer
entered the store. The bell that normally agitated me to wit's
end was a trumpet announcing the coming of a savior today!

False alarm. Just some teenager with her ugly little Chihuahua.

Again, forty-two. Forty-two. Forty-two. And the bell again.

Allison.

She had decided to wear a dress, with a little cardigan over
top of it. Under her arm she carried a folder, which I am sure
had her resume and any other forms she may have printed off
line–none of which I actually take the time to read. I scurry
back towards my office, making sure that she doesn't see me,
and walk through the door, shutting it. I rush to my desk and
sit at my computer, pretending to be busy. One of the other
associates would bring her back to me when she asked.

Let the game begin.

The knock came quietly, from obviously gentle hands. I
waited to hear a voice, assuming that one of the teenage dip-
shits had shown her where I would be. No voice came. A

knuckle tapped against the wooden door once again, this time with me responding.

"Come in," I said, trying to sound both friendly yet stern. The knob twisted and in walked the girl in the cardigan.

"Hello," she said, allowing her body to follow behind her head, inching into the office. "I was told to come in here for the interview."

"Well, you're in the right place," I said with a smile. "Why don't you have a seat and we can begin." Allison sat down at the wobbly plastic chair in front of my desk. She wiggled it for a moment, adjusting herself to find the right balance. I needed to get that damn thing fixed. Just another thing to add to the list, I suppose.

"Thank you for taking the time to see me," she said quietly, gripping the folder as it laid across her lap. "I am very excited about this interview."

"Not a problem. I like to make sure I personally sit down and chat with all of my new employee hopefuls." Obviously. I need to cool down here or I'm going to end up freaking this girl out. Take a breath. "So I have your online application here on my computer. You want to start with that and let the conversation flow from there?"

"If that's what you'd like," she replied, now lifting the folder from her lap and staring at whatever it was that was in it, leaving the pale blank cover facing towards me, obstructing my view of the papers within. I could see some color leave her face, which made me all the more curious.

"Is that your resumé?" I asked. "We can use that as a reference if you like."

"Oh, no. Sorry," Allison answered, putting the folder back on her lap. "We can use the computer. My apologies."

I paused for a moment, trying not to let her see just how much I wanted to know what was in that folder. Not for any particular reason–at least not any that made sense. I just needed to know.

"Well, would you like me to take a look at…"

"No. That's okay."

I put my outreached hand back on my desk, feeling slightly embarrassed and mildly frustrated with this response. Not letting her see my feelings, or hoping to not let her see my feelings, I smiled again, said ok, and turned back to the computer where I had her application up and ready to read. I took my first jab with a basic interview question.

"So what made you want to come work for us?"

She grinned and looked around the office a bit.

"I was always a big fan of animals and always thought it would be wonderful to spend more time with them, especially if I got to see them off into new, wonderful homes."

Of course. That was the same answer that I got from every sixteen-year-old punk who comes into this office looking for a job, I guess I shouldn't have expected anything different from this woman, even if she did have some years on the rest of the employees. I could see this interview was going to be a rather boring one after all, if it kept up at this rate. At least Allison was pretty to look at.

"I see here that you worked before at Kelly's Crafts. Is that the one just off Popple St.? I think I've been there before."

"It is."

"It seems you didn't stay there very long. Only about eight

months, unless you are still working there now, however, I see an end date on the application."

"I'm no longer working there."

"May I ask why you would leave the position?"

"I just wanted more opportunity, I suppose. I wanted to go somewhere a bit different, maybe find a job that I could actually advance in. Mom and Pop shops like Kelly's only ever have one owner, only one manager, and once they are gone, they aren't exactly going to leave their store to some out-of-the-family woman, you know? I wanted to find somewhere that I could make more money and hopefully work my way up a bit. I didn't expect that you were the type to go into Kelly's Crafts. I've never seen you around there."

This answer took me back. If anything, I could see that this woman really meant business. I felt as though I was losing control of the interview. At this point, with the answers she was giving, I certainly did not want to offer her a job. There is no way I am going to hire anyone who I think might leave in a few months, especially when she comes to find that there is no advancement in this store. The most advanced you could get was my job and I wasn't going to give that up without a fight, so unless the nine dollars an hour was step up for her, she might as well just keep moving. If it were anyone else I would've cut her free already, but I wanted to keep playing the game. I wanted to get the control back. I wanted to win, damn it.

"I should clear that up, sorry," I said. "My wife was the one who would go into the store. Not me. She was very into crafts. I wasn't exactly the artistic one, you know?"

"I see. How long has she been passed now?" Allison asked.

"I'm sorry, what?"

"Your wife. The one who came into the store. How long has it been since she passed?"

I stared at Allison, now turning my chair to face her.

"Did you know my wife? I never said anything about her passing." I said, confused.

"It's such a shame," Allison replied. "How did she go?"

There was no way in hell that this interview was going to make it to the end. I bet this woman was fired from the craft store, not quit. At this point, I realized there must be something mentally wrong with Allison. She must be off her meds or maybe one of those special folks or maybe even a drug addict or something. Regardless, she wasn't going to be working for me. No way.

"I think we need to end this conversation, ma'am," I said, keeping my head on straight but making it clear that she might as well leave.

"I don't think so. How did she pass?"

"Excuse me?" I said back, now louder. "This interview is over. Please leave."

Allison opened her folder again, looking wide-eyed at its contents. She shook her head before bringing her gaze back to me. Closing the folder, she spoke again.

"How much do you make in a year?" Allison asked me calmly.

"That is none of your business!" I responded, furiously. "I really think you need to go. If not, I'll have to call the authorities."

"That's not what you want to do," Allison smiled at me. "That's actually the last thing you want to do."

"Who the hell do you think you are?" I asked Allison. "You

must be out of your mind to think you can come in here and talk to me like this. Get out! Get out right now!"

"How much do you make in a year?" she asked again. "What's your average? We both know it isn't much. There's no shame in telling me. I'm going to find out. Just say it. How much?"

"I'm calling the police."

I grabbed the phone from the wall and dialed 911 quickly. Allison reached up and hit the receiver, ending the call before it started. I pushed her away and went to dial again, readying myself for a fight if she resisted again. Before I could press the buttons a second time, she slammed the folder onto the desk and my curiosity got the best of me. As much as I wanted this lunatic out of my office, I just as badly wanted to know what it was that she was staring at this whole time in that folder. I picked it up and slowly made my way back into my chair. She did the same.

"What's this?" I asked her, not removing my eyes from hers, thinking she might have just used it as a distraction.

"How much do you make in a year?"

I opened the folder, looked at its contents and shut it, before putting it back on the desk.

"I only make about forty thousand."

"I want thirty of it."

I began to sweat. I could feel my legs shaking.

"Where did you get these? I destroyed these."

"Apparently not all of them," Allison replied.

"Where did these come from?"

"Some boy gave them to me. Told me that I could get whatever I wanted from you with them then ran off into the store somewhere."

"A boy? What boy?" I asked.

"I don't know who he was. He was just some kid outside of the vet clinic up front. He gave them to me and as soon as I saw them, I knew he wasn't kidding. It's not like I had anything to lose–I was coming in here to beg for a minimum wage position. But I see now that he was right. I want thirty thousand of it and the job. I'm only taking thirty out of sheer kindness, which you certainly don't deserve."

I looked down at the photos in the folder again, flipping through them before getting to the resumé Allison had originally brought in, which was covered by the first draft of the suicide note; the one I had written as a test to mimic my wife's handwriting. The one that didn't turn out as well as I had wanted it to. The one I thought I had burned, but must have been wrong. I could have sworn I burned it though. This was impossible, but here it was in front of me, along with the crime photos showing my deed, which the media had deemed self-inflicted.

"What do you say?" Allison questioned me, folding her hands on the desk in front of me. I couldn't win. I couldn't fucking win. "Well?"

I closed the folder and put it down before scooting back from the table.

"Can you start on Monday?"

12

Hitch

"I always hated these damn import cars," Ruben said under his breath, kicking the tire of his Volkswagen. The car budged, making a strange ping as he withdrew his foot, pretending that he didn't kick it a little too hard, hurting his ankle in the process. "I swear, they're all pieces of shit, if you ask me. I should've gotten a Ford like my dad told me to."

"Your dad tells you to do a lot of things, bud." I replied, leaning on the guardrail. "That doesn't mean you need to listen."

Ruben's dad had always been a strange fellow. Never a bad guy. Not abusive or mean or anything like that. He had, as long as I had known him, been an idea man. At least, that is what Ruben had called it. Ever since his mom passed away–this was back when he was twelve years old or so–his dad had consistently wanted to come up with the best ways to raise his son. Much of these ideas didn't pan out the way he wanted them to. The Volkswagen was not his worst idea by a long shot.

Ruben kicked the tire again, this time with his opposite foot, before huffing off to join me on the cold steel. He folded his arms and shook his head, never breaking his vision from the large pale green steel shell that sat with its flashers on, illuminating and darkening the road around it.

"So now what?" he asked me. "Do you get cell service out here?"

I pulled my phone out of my pocket and held it towards the sky in a cinematic attempt to find bars. Nothing. The words 'No Service' sat unchanging at the top left-hand corner of the device. I shook my head to him as he walked back towards the car. The trip that we both desperately needed had turned south rather quickly. The original plan was to spend three days, two nights in a cabin out in the mountains of West Virginia, just over the state line of bordering Maryland. As soon as the road began to wind in and out and the incline began to get excitingly steep, both of our phones gave out and, unfortunately now, so did the car.

"It's probably just the alternator, Ruben. Not really a big deal," I tried. My attempt to comfort him didn't seem to take any hold. "We can just crash in the car and wait for a trooper or something to come around. Or another car. I mean, the absolute worst-case scenario would be us having to hang out until the morning and walk the road until we find service. We can't be that far out. And we have plenty of booze to keep us company in the trunk."

"I'm not trying to be stuck in the car all night, man," Ruben said back with a sulk in his voice. "This isn't the way it was supposed to happen."

He had every right to be upset. Ruben had been through a lot recently with his dad's health starting to deteriorate–he wasn't old, but cancer knows no age. It was the same thing that took his Mom. He had been in and out of hospitals for the last year, dropping weight and gaining it back pretty rapidly, throwing up for a week at a time, then be back at it within two.

Ruben needed a break and this was supposed to be it. There had always been a reason for him not to take a trip or get away before now; his dad would end up in the hospital, his semester in college would start back up, his money was too tight, and so on and so forth. German engineering was to blame this time around.

Opening the trunk and pulling two brown bottles out of the cooler that was stuffed against the edge, I reminded myself that beer just so happens to make every situation better. Including this one, I hoped. I approached Ruben as he sat on the inside of the turn, looking down the sharply slanted ditch that dragged on for hundreds of feet. I was surprised that there was no guardrail on this side of the road as opposed to the side where the mountain inclined. I felt as though the railing would be more helpful if it stopped people from driving over the edge than into the rock. I handed him the bottle and chuckled, hoping that my laugh would be contagious. It wasn't.

"It could be way worse," I said, now sitting with him on the edge.

"I suppose," he replied. It's warm out here tonight. I thought that it would be much cooler in the mountains, you know?"

"I guess it doesn't help when everything else around the mountain is pushing a hundred degrees or more. It's been a hot summer so far."

"And it's only June," Ruben said. "Damn shame the AC won't crank on without the engine. You know how hot it's going to get out here tonight?"

"Not any hotter than it is now."

"Do you think you could sleep in this? As warm as it is out

here? Even with the windows down, that car is still going to be ninety degrees or more and you know it."

He wasn't wrong. It was about ninety-five out right now and the sun had gone down about an hour ago. It wasn't going to get any cooler and we were definitely going to be stuck sleeping in some swampy, sticky air. We both started drinking from our bottles before throwing the glass down into the ditch. The sound of the breaking glass finally got Ruben to crack a smile. At least I think it was a smile I saw through the dark. We left the flashers on that night, figuring the battery was already going to have to be replaced and even if it didn't last all night, it would be safer to have it for some time than to risk getting hit by a trucker coming around the corner and not seeing us. I drifted off to sleep, watching the scene change around us from orange-tinted woods to pitch black over and over again in the front seat of the car.

We both awoke to the sound of a tapping on the car door. The flashers had stopped working and there seemed to be nothing around would but darkness.

"Hello?" said a voice from the darkness. "You boys all right?"

The voice was deep and close, coming from Ruben's side of the car. In fright, he jumped over towards my side of the car, almost into my lap.

"Whoa!" I screamed, more alarmed at his reaction than the voice.

"It's all right, boys!" the voice said, hurriedly. "I'm just checkin' to be sure you're both okay. We don't see a lot of people sleepin' on the side of the road up here and we certainly don't see too many drifters, so I figured something had to have gone wrong. The two of y'all both okay? It's a hot one out tonight."

Ruben made his way back over to his side of the car, his night vision finally coming into focus. I could begin to see the shape of a man, large in stature, leaning on the top of Ruben's broken down vehicle. He took a step back when Ruben motioned towards the handle of the car, allowing Ruben room to step out. I followed in suit, letting the unsettling breeze drift over me as I did.

"Yeah, I think we are okay," Ruben answered the man. "We were having some car trouble and figured it would be best to try to sleep on it until the morning. There isn't really any reason for us to go walking around in the dark up here. We don't know the roads that well."

"It ain't safe neither," the man said. "These ain't the kind of roads y'all would want to walk around when you can't see nothin'. That's how folks around here get themselves killed. A car come 'round that corner too fast and ain't see ya, the two of you's would be thrown clean off the mountain."

"Yeah," I said, rubbing my eyes and straightening my shoulders. "Sleeping in the car was our best bet, or so we figured."

"And you'd be right about that," said the man. "My name is Harris. But you can call me Harry. There is a shop a few miles up the road. Why don't I give you boys a lift? They open mighty early. Around six in the morning or so. By the time we get there, you'll only have to wait maybe an hour before they open up. What do ya say?"

I looked at Ruben and then over to Harry's large eighteen-wheeler parked twenty feet behind our car. Ruben shrugged his shoulders and nodded to Harry.

"That would be grea,." he said. "Thank you. We'd really appreciate the lift."

"Not a problem. Y'all just lucky I was climbing the mountain and not comin' down. Otherwise I wouldn't have been able to stop for ya." Harry said to us as he started guiding us over to his truck. "You boys ever been in a rig before?"

"Nah," I said. "I don't think so. Nothing like this."

"No worries. Just letting you know, there is a step there for you to get yourself in on. And watch your knees jumpin' in. I'd hate to see ya hurt yourself from not payin' no attention."

We climbed into the front of the truck and made our way into the cab. Ruben sat next to Harry and I slid my way into the back seat, which I assumed folded down into a mattress. There were pillows thrown up against the side and no buckle for me that I could see. Harry pulled himself into the cab directly following.

"Sorry about the mess back there, young fella," Harry said to me. "I've been out for some time now. Should be stopping for a few nights in the next town over. Normally I clean up when I hit a station. Looks like you drew the short straw."

"It's not so bad," I answered back. "You don't mind that I move these pillows and stuff, do you?"

"Not at all. *Mi casa es su casa.*" Harry laughed at his cliché and buckled himself into his seat.

Harry didn't seem to be too dirty of a guy. In fact, from my knowledge of truckers, which was minimal at best, only supported by stereotypes and television programs, he seemed to be rather clean. Even the back of his rig, that he apologized for, was cleaner than some of the better days my dorm room had seen back at school. There was no foul smell or lingering, curious waft of thick air in the truck. The AC had been on for quite some time and I was the one who actually should feel bad, pushing my sweaty back up against the seat that was obviously this man's bed. Hopefully he would be able to clean it when he hit the station he was talking about. And hopefully I didn't leave any type of wet spot or stain.

The truck started back up the mountain with a vengeance. I had never been in a vehicle with so much push to it before–not on the ground, at least. I can kind of see why guys get into this sort of thing. These machines could haul ass. Some of the turns we took certainly were what I would consider questionable, but we trusted Harry in that he knew what he was doing. If he wasn't experienced, he sure made us believe that he was.

The sun hadn't started cresting over the mountaintops yet, but I could see Ruben straining his eyes over the hills when they came into view, looking for that light just as carefully as I was. We didn't feel like we were in danger or that we needed to worry, but being able to see more than a few feet in front of us–beyond the lights of Harry's truck–would calm both of our nerves just a little.

"You boys don't mind if I play some tunes, do ya?" Harry asked us after a few moments of silence in the cab.

"Not at all," Ruben said. "By all means. Feel free. It won't bother us. I mean, you're the one doing us a favor, you know?"

With permission granted, Harry snarked a bit at Ruben's reply before twisting one of the old knobs on the dashboard, starting up some sort of 1980s metal. Maybe a Twisted Sister B-Side or something. Nothing that I had heard before and truthfully not something I think I would care to hear outside of this situation. But Ruben was right. We had no reason to complain.

The ride kept on for about fifteen more minutes before the music was broken by Ruben's voice.

"So where exactly are we headed?" he asked. "Is it like a town or just a shop somewhere?"

"It's just one of them stand-alone type shops. You don't see many towns up here in the hills. Nothin' really springs up. Ain't no water. Most towns try to come up 'round water if it can help it. Makes thing easier for the folks who live in them. This guy just owns a little station and store. No gas or nothin'. Probably not worth getting the tankers to come up there. Not enough customers, I assume. But he should have a phone for you to use." Harry smiled to Ruben, who was satisfied enough with the answer.

"So did you grow up around here, Harry?" he asked, trying to bring up a new topic to drown over the squealing guitars and repetitive bass-snare-bass-snare drum patterns. "Not like here in the mountains, but in West Virginia."

"Matter-of-fact, I did," Harry answered. "Not too far from this shop. Known the owner my whole life, practically. He's a good friend, which is why I know he won't mind helping y'all out with your little car troubles. I see him every time I make my way through these parts, here."

"Oh, that's great," Ruben commented. "Any family up this way too?"

"Nope. Just Robbie up at the shop. Y'all gon' like him. He's good people. Knows how to have a good time."

I didn't know exactly what he meant by that, but I just figured he meant some good-ole-boy banter. Maybe Robbie liked to drink and party. Either way, this early in the morning, I couldn't imagine anyone really wanting to have a good time unless that good time was a cup of coffee and maybe some food.

The digital clock on the dashboard showed 5:17 AM when we arrived at the tiny, run-down looking building off the main road. The truck came to a stop in front of it, making a screech as Harry pulled a lever down, which I assumed was an emergency brake.

"We here, boys," Harry exclaimed. "You two stay right here. Let me see if ole Robbie is in the building already."

None of the lights were on through the windows. When Harry left the truck, Ruben and I shared a look of confusion before he shrugged his shoulders and pushed his head back into the headrest of the chair.

"I really hope this guy has a phone," Ruben said to me, still looking through the giant glass windshield into the darkness. "I'd really like to get this weekend started."

"Me too," I shared. "And maybe get us out of this not-so-settling part of the woods." I laughed a little at my own comment, but didn't receive the same reaction from Ruben. He just stared straight ahead, breathing deeply.

We waited for a few more minutes, sitting in the quiet, listening to the small sounds of the woods around us; crickets mostly. I thought I could hear a bird chirping off somewhere, but I think my mind wanted the sun to be up and was allowing my ears to hear whatever I wanted to hear. Ruben restlessly undid his seat belt.

"I'm going to go see what's going on," he said, reaching

around the door for the handle. "I don't want to just sit around. I'm not getting anything done just sitting here."

"I don't think Harry forgot about us or anything, Rube," I replied. "Just relax a little."

"Nah, man. I need to stretch a bit anyways. Besides, don't you want to meet Robbie? I hear he is good people and knows how to have a good time. Weren't you listening?"

I chuckled under my breath at the remark, still not feeling confident about Ruben leaving the truck.

"I don't know, bud," I said.

"Stop," Ruben cut me off. "It's fine. I'll walk up, if I see Harry I'll ask what's up. If I see Robbie, I'll ask about the phone. I'm sure it isn't an issue. Shit, if he has anything to eat in that store, I might even grab a snack. If there is, do you want anything?"

"No thanks. I'm all right," I shook my head. "I'm just going to try to rest up a bit if you're going to handle this."

"Sounds good to me," Ruben said. "I'll be right back." The door shut loudly behind him and I lost sight of his shape as he made his way into the darkness behind the shop. Not being able to see him made my stomach cramp up. I shook it off, closed my eyes, and put my head back against the seat.

The moving of the cab woke me up from a shallow sleep. There was still no lights, but the driver's side of the truck weighed down as Harry climbed back into the vehicle.

"Hey, Harry," I said, rubbing my eyes and sitting up straight. "Everything good?"

"Yes, sir," he said back. "Everything is right as rain."

"Awesome," I said softly. "Where is Ruben? I assume Robbie was able to help us? Did he have a phone?"

"Naw. But he decided to do you boys one better. He's fixin'

to grab that car of yours with his tow and bring it on back to the shop for ya. Fix it up there and all. Shouldn't take him more than a day. He knows his way around a vehicle."

"That's amazing. Thank you, Harry," I excitedly replied. "Where is Ruben?"

"He went ahead with Robbie in the tow truck to show him where the car is sittin'. We are gonna head back that way ourselves now."

Harry had to have seen the confused look on my face because he turned around, patted me on the knee, and smiled before flipping on the engine of the truck and putting it in gear. The clock on the dash now shined 5:49 AM at me in its green, pale light. It was the only thing that gave any color to the inside the cab.

We drove down the road for a few moments when I was finally able to see the sun starting to come up over the crest. The pink and yellow hue filled the area around us, just enough for me to notice some of the details in the back seat, where I had remained even though Ruben had gone with Robbie, leaving the front seat up for grabs. The seat itself was tightly covered in a dark sheet and on the floor I saw what seemed to be a dozen or so photographs. I leaned down to pick them up and scooped them into my hand. Harry didn't take his eyes off the road. As I sifted through the pictures, I realized that they were all of kids. Each photograph had an image of a single child, ranging anywhere from nine or ten years to their late teens. All of them seemed to be scared or confused, their expressions that of discomfort. All except one–the one of a young, pale man, possibly the youngest in the bunch, with incredibly blue eyes. He was smiling a huge, almost sinister grin.

"What are these, Harry?" I asked, holding the pictures up so he could see them in the rearview mirror. "Family or something?"

He peered back for a minute, his expression not changing, staying straight-faced and stone-like.

"Yeah," he said. "Something like that." He then went back to driving, not caring in the slightest to mention what he meant by 'something like that.'

We pulled up to the car and Harry put the truck in park before stepping out, not saying a word. He walked back around the cabin and towards the back of the rig. I stared at the pictures again and realized yet another similarity. Each of the photos happened to be taken in the same place. With the light now coming through the windows, I could make things out more clearly. The pictures were taken from above the children, who were either sitting or maybe kneeling next to the photographer. The floor they were sitting on was grey, much like steel, and seemed to be ridged somehow. I looked closer, holding the photographs up towards the window. On the ridges in the floor seemed to be rivets. That is when it dawned on me.

The pictures were all taken in the back of the truck, inside the large container that was hitched to the cab.

I look up from the picture to reach for the door, only to find Harry standing in front of me, no emotion at all. I quickly gaze out the windshield and realize that neither Ruben or Robbie or any other vehicle was around us, other than the car. I jumped out the other side of the cab and ran around to the front, placing my hand on the hood of the mechanical beast.

"Where's Ruben, Harry?" I asked with force. "Where is he?"

"I told you, son," Harry replied with ease and stillness in his voice. "He is with Robbie. Robbie got him. I got you."

"What the hell is that supposed to mean?" I blurted out, now starting to sweat from both fear and heat of the morning air. "Where is he? You said they'd be here!"

"Calm down, little man," Harry commanded, raising his tone as he took a step towards me. "Ruben is in good hands. And so are you. Now come around to the back of the truck. I want to show you something."

I pushed off the front of the truck and scurried backwards towards the Volkswagen, bumping it with my calves when I reached it.

"Who were the people in the pictures? Why were they in your rig? Who took them? You?"

"You ask a lot of questions, bud. Come here." Harry kept moving towards me, looming slowly and patiently. "I don't want it say it again."

Harry was only a few feet from me as I scooted across the hood of the Volkswagen towards the mountainside. The ditch led a long way down–steep and dreadful into the valley hundreds of feet below.

"Get back!" I yelled, my feet touching the edge. "Get away from me!"

Harry smiled.

"Ain't nowhere for you to go, son." he said, menacingly. "Now be a good little boy and get your ass over here."

Without thinking, I turned and jumped down the hill and into the valley. I began to roll as I lost my balance and continued to do so, bouncing off trees and rocks. I could feel my flesh tearing with every flip my body made. I finally stopped after skidding across concrete. It was there that I blacked out.

When I awoke, a police officer was kneeling over me, his hand attempting to read a pulse on my throat.

"Well good heavens, kid! You're awake!" he said with excitement. Reaching over to his shoulder and grabbing his radio, he said something in a deep southern drawl that I could barely understand. I just heard a slew of numbers and the words 'found boy.' Within a few minutes an ambulance was there to take me to the local hospital. The police took my statement about the man in the truck but had no answers.

The next morning, I got to have a conversation with my mother at the hospital. I told her that they had found me on the side of the road and that I had fallen down into the valley. I told her about my broken legs and rib, and told her about the cuts and bruises. I left out the part about the trucker. It wasn't for her to know yet. She doesn't deserve to worry about it. Not until I am back home in Maryland, at least, where she knows I will be safe.

A new officer I hadn't seen before came by, bringing me some of the things from the Volkswagen. He brought me my bag that had clothes, something I could change into since the shirt and jeans I was wearing before were completely destroyed in the fall. He brought me some of the small bags of chips from the back seat and a few water bottles, which I was incredibly grateful for, seeing as how I would be in the hospital for a few more days. He also handed me a folder with all of the vehicle's information from the glove box. I opened the folder to look at the paperwork and pulled out a print of a photograph. That was what made my heart stop.

"Where did you get this?" I asked the officer. "Where was this?"

"It was on the windshield of your car." the officer said back. "Under the wipers. I threw it in the folder in case you wanted it."

"It isn't my car," I said, my eyes glued to the picture.

"Then whose is it?" the officer asked.

I held up the picture for him to see. The picture showed Ruben, scared, sitting on the ridged and riveted floor of the truck container.

"It's his."

13

Andrew

Andrew's skin burned as they pulled the noose tightly around his neck. He choked back tears and feverishly searched the crowd for some face of mercy but found none amongst the scowls of the townsfolk who wanted nothing more than to see his nine-year-old body dangle from atop the gallows' angled posts. The executioner worried how quickly such a tiny young man would perish, given that his weight may not be enough to break the bones that held his head when he dropped, but was hurriedly forced to set the execution, with or without his own consent. The people knew what they wanted and that was to watch Andrew's legs kick as he made worthless attempts for air in the center of the town.

The townspeople had impatiently waited for the day that vengeance was granted. They all stood with smiles as they were about to be able to justify the horrors of the past few months, though this was not the outcome that they had originally expected. But they had their proof, or so they thought, that would make everything they were about to witness worth the trouble and worth the pull of the hangman's lever. This boy, this baby of a boy, had to die where he stood and one second later would be one second too late. He needed to perish in front of those he had offended and he needed to be able to count the teeth in their mouths as they grin from ear to ear at his demise, this public spectacle as it were. They gleamed at his screams and cries for help, all knowing that he would not receive any sort of grace from this crowd. No, they stood and heard him holler out for his parents, whom he knew damn well were already dead, as if they would save him through some divine intervention if they hadn't already been torn to pieces in the bowels of Hell for birthing such a horrendous creature as Andrew. The audience let out a cheer when the noose was slid down tight towards the back of his head, causing his cries to halt for just a moment, pinching the way for oxygen to reach his lungs. This would be first step on his route to the grave, which was shallowly dug outside of the city walls.

This is what fate had in store for young Andrew, first and only born of his now-deceased parents, friend to none, menace to all.

Andrew was born just before the turn of the twentieth century, a gritty period for most, to a family of only two, a loving man and wife. Andrew's parents cared deeply for him and considered themselves lucky that Andrew never wanted for much because they would more than likely never been able to give him much to begin with. There was no great wealth in Andrew's family, no inheritance or family treasure passed down the line. In fact, the only thing they still had from their parents, Andrew's grandparents, was a small leather-bound family Bible in which they used to conduct their Sunday prayers. The book was worth nothing, just like their home, their clothing, and the rest of their scattered belongings. The only thing that they owned of any true value to them or the world was young Andrew, the cutest boy that could have ever been born with the bluest of eyes you could have never foreseen.

When Andrew turned nine years old, his parents saved up every penny that they had and they bought Andrew his first bicycle. He would ride it up and down the dirt roads by his house, smiling and laughing with every kick of the pedal. He loved the bike more than anything in the world and couldn't wait to wake up every morning just so he could go outside and ride it to school, which his parents allowed just as long as he came straight home when he was finished. Andrew was a tiny young man, fairly skinny and much shorter than the rest of the boys his age. While they would all play ball outside in the school courtyard, Andrew would sit and watch from a distance, knowing that if he ever approached the other boys to play along, it would end with nothing but relentless teasing and ridicule, possibly even some physical injury. Andrew knew that it was much safer just to sit by his bicycle and watch them all play their games. So that is was he did, every single day, without ever saying a word to anyone otherwise.

Andrew was a brilliant young academic. His parents had raised him to understand just how important a good education was and assured him that if he studied, he could make it far in life, maybe even find some type of job where he could make real money like some of the other boys' parents. Andrew didn't think or care much for money but knew that he wanted to see his mother and father happy, so when he got home from school, he would spend quite some time with his face in a book learning about the different ways that the world worked, hoping to see something that interested him so he could converse about it with his parents over supper which mostly consisted of a mush that his mother had thrown together in the old large cauldron that was kept over the wooden stove. His parents, not nearly as bright as their son, would smile and nod and make sure he believed that they understood the things he read, which they certainly did not seeing as how neither of them could read themselves.

Both of Andrew's parents grew up in the country and were poorer than they are now. Andrew's father spent his youth working as a farmhand instead of going to school like most of the other boys and decided not to join the military, even though he knew that it was some sort of passage for folks his age around the time he met Andrew's mother. She was only a few years younger than he and also from a family that got most of their income from the farmland they watched over. She would do the odd chores around the house and had slightly more education that Andrew's father, but not much. She had stopped running to the schoolhouse up the road when she was about twelve while Andrew's father stopped at ten. Lillian, Andrew's mother, would recollect on the one and only time a truancy officer actually had the nerve to approach her father about his daughter's absence from the class. She told Andrew that the man got out almost two full sentences before her father told him that Lillian was his daughter and he would make all the decisions for her. He told the man that if he ever came up to the house again looking for his daughter that we would be greeting the Lord that very same day with the help of a steel long rifle that was kept above the fireplace of their home. The man tipped his hat and was off, never to be seen again.

The other kids at Andrew's school would pick on him from

time to time about being a teacher's pet and knowing all of the answers. He got good marks on account of all of his studying, and by the time he turned nine, he had become too embarrassed and afraid to answer the questions asked by his teachers. He sat silently, just as he did in the courtyard, and let the other boys take stabs at the questions, of which many would fail to answer correctly. He didn't have any friends, his parents lacked the intelligence he had, and the world rejected this impoverished young man even more so than he realized in his humble youth. Life was hard for Andrew. Life showed him no mercy. Life, as Andrew saw it, was a shameful, awful thing.

By the time Andrew's folks had noticed Andrew's grades were beginning to slip, their home life had gone even farther into decline. There were debts that urgently needed to be paid which his parents could not afford and there were men regularly banging on the rugged and patched wooden door of their tiny home. Andrew knew never to answer the door for these men and his parents would sit in silence, just listening to the angry voices holler insults from outside about them needing payment. Something needed to be done or Andrew felt that they would tear the door down–and he didn't want to see what would happen if they ever actually made it through that door. He was wise enough to know it would not be good for his mother and father. So every night, Andrew did the only thing he knew he could do that might shine some light on the situation: he prayed.

Andrew prayed hard and would force his eyes closed so tightly that he would see spots upon opening them again. He would run his knees raw from shuffling back and forth on them at the edge of the mat that he called his bed. Sometimes he would pray out loud and other times he would pray as quietly as he could, hoping not to disturb his parents as they slept. He prayed every single day for months, but nothing ever came of it. At least, not until the week he was to die.

One evening, after his prayers had been muttered, Andrew fell asleep, on the edge of tears, but remaining composed for nobody but himself. The drift into unconsciousness was not an easy one, but he was greeted by a dream of grassy fields as he entered. Andrew stood in the middle of the field and looked over the horizon where he could, just barely, if he squinted hard enough, see the shadow of a man in the distance. He began to walk towards this figure, tall and thin, only to see that he was dressed in the nicest suit jacket that Andrew had ever seen. As he approached the man, he felt a sense of intimidation overwhelm him and he staggered back, tripping on his own feet, landing on his hind end. He scurried backwards as the man returned the approach with one of his own, taking leisurely steps towards Andrew, whose hands were now dirty from the rich soil of the fields. The man reached down, grabbing Andrew's wrist, and lifted him to his feet, dusting off his shoulders with a quick and effortless motion.

Andrew peered at the man's face and was horrified to see that this creature had no features. Nothing but a black complexion in the shape of its head sitting on its shoulders surrounding what Andrew could only assume were two pure white eyes. Andrew stood frozen, staring at the creature with wide eyes. Though this thing had no lips, Andrew could hear it speak with a deep, rumbling voice that seemed to shake the ground beneath his feet.

"What troubles you?" it said to him, returning one hand to

its side as the other sat firm on Andrew's upper arm, almost as if to comfort him.

"Wh-what do you mean?" Andrew replied softly, dreading the reaction that might come from this creature if questioned. He felt the grip on his arm begin to loosen.

"You're troubled, young man. I can help you. What can I do? How may I help you?" it said to Andrew, not moving from its straight, slender position. Andrew searched the area where the creature's face should be, trying to see any sign that this thing was human, but failed at the task with anguish. As not to upset the thing, he responded.

"My troubles are simple and yet incredibly complex." The being showed no reaction to this, remaining still and silent. "My family is poor, I have no friends, and the world seems to be playing a cruel, cruel trick on me. Every time I feel like we have lost everything, something else goes missing from our lives–or rather, is taken away. There isn't anything you or any-one can do though. It is just the life we live. This is where we are and where we will remain, I'm sure."

The creature lowered his grip from Andrew's arm and stood as a statue in front of him. The rumble from his voice made Andrew's joints tremble on their hinges.

"There is nothing I can't fix. Nothing I can't resolve," it said. "Are these the things you want to see change in your life? Will these things make you happy?"

"Who are you?" Andrew finally built up the courage to ask, trying to sneak an inch further away from the thing with every few seconds. "What do you want from me?"
"I am here to help you, Andrew," it replied. "I am here to make everything better."

"But what do you want from me?" Andrew asked, nervously awaiting some response, which he assumed would only be some ridiculous cost that he couldn't afford. He knew very well that there was nothing he could offer, so even the fewest of cents, the smallest of coins, would be too expensive for his blood. He had nothing to give.

"I want you to carry on the deed," the thing said in its low grumble. "I do for you, and you do for others. It is that simple. Is that something you can do?"

Andrew took stock of this. He had no idea what the dark figure meant, but he did know that he would be grateful enough, if brought out of poverty, to pass on the aid to anyone he could. Andrew knew that he was good enough of a man for the job and, if only he had the push, much like this creature was offering him, he would be able to change the lives of other people just like him.

"What are you?" Andrew questioned. "Why me? How?"

"Consider me a friend," it replied. "Simply a friend–one who wants to help. What do you say? I help you, and you continue to help others. Sound like a deal?"

Andrew stepped towards the thing and cautiously held out his tiny hand.

"Deal," he said, waiting for the figure to extend a hand as well. Though he could not see it, Andrew could feel the thing smiling. With a flash, Andrew was pushed backwards by what seemed like a flash of light. The sound seemed to rattle his eardrums and occurred to him as nothing more than a *thud*–the same sound he had heard when the bullies at school would box his ears, but much, much louder. His eyes shut and he felt his bottom land on the dirt where the grass used to be.

He slid on his back, the small stones dragging up under his shirt, tearing at his skin. There was immediate regret in his decision to make this deal.

Andrew woke up screaming.

His parents rushed from their bed to his side, asking him if everything was ok and if he had heard something in the night. He told them about his dream and they shook their heads, telling him that maybe he needed to refrain from some of the fiction he read before he went to sleep. He insisted that the dream was not fueled by any stories or anything he had heard or engaged in before and that everything that happened felt so real. He ran his hand across his back, expecting torn flesh, but there was nothing there but his soft, sweating flesh. His parents recommended that he go back to sleep so that he would be able to get up proper in the morning to get to the schoolhouse. Andrew didn't fall back asleep and spent the rest of those early morning hours trying to understand what it was that his brain had just conjured up.

The following week went by like every other. Andrew would wake (when he could sleep well enough), go to school, sit quietly, then come home. He thought about the change the figure in his dreams had promised and wondered if anything would ever come of it. Day in and day out, nothing happened–his family was still poor, he still had no friends, and the world, just as he had mentioned in the dream, was still playing along with the cruel trick it had begun at Andrew's birth.

As Andrew carried his books to school the week after, he had just about forgotten that the dream had even existed. He chalked it up to silly figments of his imagination and even believed that maybe, somewhere in his reading, he had come up with the idea of this figure, well-dressed in his Sunday best but that looked like it belonged nowhere near a church. He was almost to the schoolhouse, the peak of the small wooden steeple sitting just outside of his view when there was a heavy tug on his arm. Dropping his books, Andrew was yanked into an alley where he received a sharp pain across the back of his head, right at the base of his skull. He blacked out, hearing a thud similar to that in his dream as he fell into the darkness.

———————

They hanged the man that grabbed Andrew. He hanged by his neck after a short drop from the pedestal of the gallows, his legs kicking wildly as his mouth opened and closed, failing to capture his last final breaths of air. Andrew had not been the first child this man had come across–and used–before his capture only a day after he had taken Andrew. The bodies of many young men from around the county were found buried low beneath the floorboards of his home, covered by many layers of dirt and stone. This man had been very careful in his ways not to be caught by any type of authority, but luckily for Andrew, a small girl had been looking from her window just down the dirt road a ways and told her daddy that there was man attacking a boy she had seen walking the path many times before. The police where able to track the man down from the girl's description and, within forty-eight hours, had the bastard's feet swinging over the pit.

Andrew, though in pain–both physically and emotion-ally–had received the word of this man's inheritance with glee. The kidnapper, being the deviant man that he was never took a bride and, in that respect, had also never given birth to any children. When it was discovered that this man had no liv-ing family and was nothing more than some common con man, they decided to give the assets of his small estate–a few hundred dollars and the house in which the man lived–to Andrew, the only surviving victim. Andrew gave the money to his parents who promptly paid their debts and immediately moved into the house. Andrew shivered at the idea of staying in a house–one with such a morbid history–but his parents reminded him that this was a blessing and that he should be more open-minded to the whole situation. He was shocked at the attitude his parents had taken since finding their way out of debt. He insisted that they sell the house and maybe move into another that was just as decent, but his parents informed him that no one would want to buy a house owned by a lunatic and that this was a gift from God himself. They were given everything they needed to survive and more and that Andrew should be grateful. But he wasn't. Andrew spent many nights in that house crying alone in his bedroom–the first he had ever had to himself.

Andrew's schoolmates treated him differently when he returned to school. They felt sorry for him, knowing that he was damaged now and though they had never been inviting to him before, chose to be sympathetic, asking Andrew to play in their courtyard games after classes and insisting that he join them during meals. It was all so very fake and forced and Andrew had no problem figuring out that none of the attention that he was getting from the fellow children was genuine. Andrew was still just as lonely as he was before, but now had more chatter in his ear. He began to miss the way things were before. He wanted nothing more than to be left alone with his books in the small shack he had always called home, instead of the house of a rapist and murderer, bothered by the voices and pity from the rest of the town. Andrew awaited the chance to speak with the dark figure again so he may plead for his old life back. That moment came sooner than Andrew expected.

In the lush green fields just as before, Andrew was not afraid as the statuesque creature approached him. Andrew stood up to the thing and called out to him in the most demanding voice his meek body could offer.

"Take it all back!" Andrew called to him, his fist clenched at his side. "Take all of it! I don't want this life anymore!"

The thing didn't move but rumbled its voice in an all too familiar tone.

"You are not pleased?" it asked Andrew. "This is everything that you wanted, is it not? You have no more poverty, a new home, new friends–everything that a young man could wish for. The new world has been given to you. Are you not grateful?"

"This isn't what I wanted. None of it," Andrew said back. "The friends aren't real, the house is a reminder of my nightmare, and the money has done nothing but support my parents' lack of affection. Please, sir, please, I beg you. Take it all away."

The figure reached out and placed its limb on Andrew's' shoulder, as it had before.

"But child, we had a deal," it replied. "A man cannot back down from his deal. His word must be his bond, you understand."

"I will hold up my end. I will! Somehow. Just give me back the life I had before, a life untainted by such horrors."

"And you will continue to carry out the good deed?" the creature asked.

"Yes. I swear it," said Andrew, now sounding smaller than ever with every word that left his lips. "I swear."

Within seconds, the *thud* and light hit him hard again and he was back in his bedroom. He stood to find that nothing had changed. Disappointed, he fell back asleep, this time without crying, faithful that change would soon come.

He awoke to a banging on the front door of the house, which seemed all too much like that from the shack which he used to live in, back when the men would pound the doors to collect the money they were owed. The slamming continued as and Andrew could hear the muffled hollers from a man on the other side of the wood. He rushed down the hallway and into the small foyer where he swung the door open to find an officer there, baton in hand. The officer pushed Andrew aside and entered the home asking what had happened just a few minutes ago. Andrew had no idea what he was talking about, but was informed that one of the neighbors had reported screaming just moments before and that the boy had to have heard it.

When Andrew shrugged, the large man pushed Andrew aside once again and headed down the hall, opening each door as he went. When he entered the room belonging to

Andrew's parents he let out a gasp before vomiting a small puddle there in the hallway. He approached Andrew, turned him around, and quickly bound his hands together. Other officers came to the house shortly following the discovery of his parents' corpses. They also found the bloodied knife laying under Andrew's pillow which was apparently used to mutilate the bodies beyond any recognition. Andrew pleaded with the officers that he hadn't done it, but the evidence suggested otherwise. He even tried to tell them about the dream, but they insisted that he was mad and making up stories. They dragged him from the house and threw him into a cell, only slightly smaller than the shack which he used to live in and, just as before, he had no money and no friends. Just like he had asked for.

———————

Andrew stood patiently, yet nervously, for the executioner to pull the lever that would drop him into the hole below the stage. They had to stack books up on top of the platform for Andrew to stand on seeing as how there hadn't been enough slack on the rope and they were not going to waste the time retying a knot for the likes of him. Andrew could hear the priest, standing off to his right, whispering a prayer. A hush fell over the crowd, the books dropped, the noose tightened, and Andrew felt the blood rush to his face, pushing his eyes forward in his skull. He kicked his feet and tried to catch his breath as he dangled above the ground but failed at both attempts. The crowd never said a word as he suffered. The world went dark after what Andrew could've guessed was a minute or so.

His eyes opened again in the field and he was standing before the figure. It reached out to grab Andrew's shoulder.

"Just as I helped you, you will help others. You will carry on the deed, from one friend to another."

Andrew looked around, realizing what had become of him, and nodded his head.

About the Author

M.J. Orz is an author and blogger from Baltimore, MD. He runs HorrorFictionBlog.com and has been featured on Podcasts such as The NoSleep Podcast, Night Fears Podcasts, Mr. CreepyPasta, and The Phantom Librarian.

Thought Catalog, it's a website.
www.thoughtcatalog.com

Social
facebook.com/thoughtcatalog
twitter.com/thoughtcatalog
tumblr.com/thoughtcatalog
instagram.com/thoughtcatalog

Corporate
www.thought.is

www.ingramcontent.com/pod-product-compliance
Lightning Source LLC
Chambersburg PA
CBHW020328200626
46814CB00006BB/2470